KIDNAPPED BY THE GENTLEMAN

GENTLEMAN'S BOUNTY: BOOK ONE

DRAKE LAMARQUE

GREY KELPIE STUDIO

CHAPTER 1

KINGSTON, JAMAICA - 1720 SEPTEMBER

I woke up suddenly, heart racing as if a door had slammed or someone had shouted, startling me. I couldn't remember dreaming, perhaps I had heard something in the real world, but I was distracted from what it could have been by a thumping pain in my head and various aches in my body. I was lying face down... somewhere.

Groaning, I tried to remember the night before. It was largely a blur. The taste in my mouth was of stale wine and tobacco smoke, which told me I had been drinking, perhaps at a party. Hardly surprising.

It seemed as if I were on a bed, at least, something large and flat and comfortable. The fabric under my hands felt like a bedsheet.

I couldn't tell if I was alone in the bed, or not.

I rubbed my eyes, dislodging an alarming amount of dry, sandy sleep from them. Finally, I dared to open my eyes a crack, which hurt because there was bright morning sunlight streaming in from somewhere. Somewhere high up.

I groaned again, and there was a responding noise from nearby. My eyes flew open and I pushed myself up on my hands to look around. I instantly winced, closing my eyes again, because there was a pain over my back.

What on Earth did I get up to last night?

The other person sighed again, making the kind of 'let me sleep' noise I was accustomed to making myself when a servant came to wake me for breakfast. I forced my eyes open to, at the very least, identify who it was making the noises.

There were, apparently, several people sleeping nearby. So the question wasn't so much 'who' as 'how many?'

The room was unfamiliar, but slowly memories started to return. The Hellfire Club. The mysterious and scandalous secret society, which I'd managed to snag an invitation to. The Masquerade, that's what I'd come for. A masquerade the night before...

Must've drunk too much and passed out.

Or done something else.

I looked down at myself. Yes, I was indeed naked.

Right, find your clothes, that's the first step. Clothes. Dressing yourself is the next step, and then get out. They might try to tell you they love you or some ridiculous thing like that.

A small voice in the back of my head suggested I might be concerned that I couldn't remember the night before or where I was, but the ache in my head had been joined by a sharp pain in my throat.

From the quality of light (bright) and the taste in my mouth (stale), I deduced it must be morning.

Probably Oliver would be worried about me. I should get back.

I rubbed my hand over my forehead before hauling myself up off the bed and pulling my trousers on. I winced a little at the movement, I was aching all over.

Probably just means I had a really good night.

I had no idea where the peacock mask I'd worn the night

before had gone, but fuck it. Not like I was about to wear it again.

No, the next thing I needed was my shirt. Where was my shirt? I found it crumpled on the floor, and picked it up. I pulled it on with trembling hands. My skin hurt.

Why does my skin hurt? Must've... maybe there are scratches down my back from some particularly rough love making?

I buttoned my shirt and walked to the door, picking over the sleeping forms, careful not to wake anyone.

My head pounded with each step, and my eyes blurred. What had I been drinking the night before?

When I got to the door, I tried to turn the handle and open it but it was locked. Which did seem curious, but not exactly unheard of for a party where people had been doing such debauched and fun things.

I felt in the pocket of my trousers but found nothing there.

I looked around for a key but it made my head spin to do so.

The nearest sleeping form, of which there were perhaps three or four, but one had her hair in what must have been an elaborate coiffure. It had somewhat fallen down now, but it was partially held a hairpin in the shape of an orchid.

I exhaled, trying to steady my vision, then leaned in and plucked it from her hair. I didn't breathe, in case she woke, but all that happened was the golden coils of her locks uncoiled prettily over her bare neck. I watched for a moment, transfixed until it settled.

Time is of the essence. I need to get back home, to Oliver.

I did hate to make Oliver worry, but well. He worried about me plenty, I'm sure, but I hated to make him *proper* worried.

I took a deep breath, steeled myself, and using the hairpin I picked the lock in the door. This was a skill I had learned by necessity back in London. Back there, I'd had too many lovers who had spouses fond of suddenly returning without warning.

Quick escapes were important to be able to accomplish with minimal tools.

The door's lock clicked and I pushed the door open before setting the pin down next to its owner. Whatever else I was, I wasn't a thief.

It seemed I was in some sort of cellar, as the landing was small and dark, and largely dominated by a set of stairs.

I took the stairs up, found myself in the foyer of the grand house the masquerade party had been held in. In the absence of any servants, and hardly wanting to attract attention, I showed myself out.

I was halfway up the road before I realised shoes or boots may have been a good idea. My feet began to hurt on the rough cobbles, but it was just another pain on top of the pounding in my head, the aches in my limbs and the weird way my skin itself hurt.

At least it wasn't far to get home.

Kingston was such a *little* town after all. I spared a glance up the hill at the Governor's house, where there had been a fancy to-do the night before - one I'm sure my father would have wanted me to attend with all the finest of ex-London society, but instead, I'd gone to the party at the Hellfire Club.

It was somewhat curious that I'd fallen asleep there... usually, I favoured slipping out on my lovers in the early hours of the morning and sleeping at home. Curious.

But I'd made a clean escape, and I felt sure there was nothing to worry about.

CHAPTER 2

⁂

IN WHICH CEDRIC RETURNS TO THE TOWNHOUSE

*T*he house was in a bit of uproar, which was unusual for a... what day was it? Thursday? I had no idea. It was unusual.

I let myself in the front door - the townhouse was small but well-appointed, rented by my father to house me in my exile. There were three maids, a cook and a valet as well as Oliver of course.

My heart did its usual little flutter when I thought of how soon I'd be seeing Oliver again.

Stupid, foolish heart. It will never come to anything. I know that. And yet, the heart continues to yearn.

I hurried up the stairs to my room, which was in the process of being cleaned by the maid, Ionie. I hesitated in the doorway, realising with some surprise that she wasn't simply cleaning, she was packing some of my things into my travelling chest.

Now why would she be doing that?

I cleared my throat and Ionie looked up at me with a surprised expression.

"Master Cedric! You must hurry," she said.

"I must hurry for what, exactly?"

"You don't know?"

I felt a hand on my shoulder, which made me startle. I hadn't heard anyone behind me. Of course, my head was still throbbing with pain and there was an unpleasant ringing noise in my ears, so I don't think I *could* have heard anyone behind me, but I startled all the same.

"Cedric?"

Oliver. I turned to look at him, my mouth going dry all over again. He was as pretty as ever. His wire rimmed glasses a little grubby as usual, hiding the brightness of his azure eyes.

"Good morning, oh tutor of mine," I said, trying for mischievous charm.

From Oliver's curled lip and raised eyebrows, it came across as slightly mania-fuelled.

"Good morning, where have you been all night? Or shouldn't I ask?" He rubbed his thumb against my back, which felt impossibly uncomfortable, not from the intimacy of the gesture which frankly I appreciated, but somehow his touch stung. He saw my flinch and quickly dropped his hand. "Sorry."

"No, it's nothing, I was simply... out at a party. What's going on, why is Ionie packing my paintings and paints?"

"A letter arrived late yesterday afternoon. You're... well, *we're* asked to return to London," Cedric said. He had a piece of paper in his other hand, I recognised the fluid script my father used. My throat tightened, and I winced at the feeling.

"Asked to return? But surely he doesn't mean right this minute?" I swallowed and plucked the paper from his hand, scanning the words and feeling doom settle upon my shoulders.

The letter wasn't addressed to me, of course, I couldn't be trusted with matters of... myself.

Instead, it was directed to Oliver, the perfect, well-behaved good boy that he was.

Mister Stanhope,

I trust this letter finds you well.

Reports of Cedric's continued misbehaviour have reached us here in London. His mother is terribly upset and I myself am beyond disappointed.

We had hoped sending Cedric away from the bad influences in London would improve his disposition. This, as you know, is why we engaged the services of an upstanding young man such as yourself.

In order to keep a firmer rein on Cedric's misadventures, I have no choice but to insist on his immediate return to London. I trust you to chaperone him back on the next available Naval vessel, I have enclosed a letter to the Governor to arrange this.

Once the passage is secured, I understand the Navy has some way of sending messages quickly. I should like to know when to expect my son.

Terribly sorry but please understand, under the circumstances, I cannot continue your contract as tutor for Cedric once he is back in my care. I shall, of course, pay you for all the days leading up to the one where you bring him to my door.

Yours faithfully

The Honourable Ackley Hale-Harrington, esquire

"Trust Father to use his full title when he's sending a scolding letter for the return of his son," I joked, although my heart wasn't in it. "I'm surprised he didn't add what he's currently the minister of."

"I understand that he did in the letter addressed to Governor Keene," Oliver said. His voice was a little softer than usual, he was trying to joke as well.

Poor sod's just lost his job. Thankless though it was at least it was a wage.

"Oliver, I'm so sorry about your contract," I said. I looked up to meet his startlingly blue eyes. My breath caught for a moment. "Really, I can argue with him and get your contract continued, none of this is your fault in the least."

Oliver shook his head and raised a hand, placating. "It's fine, this was never a permanent role. The fact is that he's right. I haven't been a good chaperone to you."

"You weren't supposed to be a chaperone, you were teaching me Latin and Literature, and you've done that. I've read Shakespeare, I know the difference between thee and thou, you've done well."

Oliver's gaze slid to the side and I read the letter again, an unpleasant thought occurring to me. "He hired you to do more than that, didn't he?"

Oliver didn't reply, which was, of course, all the response I needed. I sighed and went into my room. "Thank you, Ionie, I can handle the packing from here."

Ionie nodded and left the room, keeping her eyes down as she passed Oliver.

My head thumped, and now the pain was centralised directly behind my eye. I didn't want to talk about any of this. I wanted to collapse in my bed and sleep until I didn't hurt any more.

I was highly aware of Oliver lingering in the doorway of my bedroom.

"Cedric," Oliver said, his voice conciliatory. He was trying to make up, to apologise to me. I had to resist the urge to turn to him and tell him it was all right. It wasn't all right. We had to go back to London and my freedom would be severely curtailed. It wasn't Oliver's fault, but it wasn't... *not* his fault either.

I couldn't cope with this. It was too much information to take in on a day when I'd got up to God only knew what the night before. I simply couldn't be the soul of wit and politeness any longer.

"If you don't mind," I said, shorter and more abruptly than my heart truly wanted, but I'd started now, and my tongue hadn't ever known how to stop. "I'd like a moment to myself. I need to close my eyes, vomit and give in to the sweet release of death. Probably not in that order."

I took hold of the door to my room and started to close it. "Good night."

"Don't die, please," Oliver said in a small voice. Then he shook his head, bracing a hand on the door so I couldn't shut it all the way. That annoyed me. "Our ship sails at nine tonight. You must be packed and ready to go by then, Cedric."

"Nine?! *Today*?"

My mouth went even drier than it had been, which I honestly hadn't imagined was possible. My poor, tender, alcohol pickled brain scrambled to make sense of the words Oliver had said with his sweet pale pink lips.

"Today?" I said again.

"Yes, Cedric. Honestly, if you weren't so hungover perhaps you'd understand."

Oooh, now I've made him annoyed with me. Damn but he's sexy when he's pissed off. I wish he'd spank me. Maybe then I'd be able to behave...

No, I'm getting distracted. He's still talking. What's he saying? Focus, Cedric.

"- your Father made it abundantly clear. The next ship bound for London is at nine tonight. It's called the Trinity Royal and the captain has agreed to take us on as passengers."

"Oh for fuck's sake."

I closed the door on him. Partially, so he'd stop talking and partially so I didn't just abandon all sense of pride and throw myself into his pleasantly muscular arms and ask him to make it all better somehow.

I didn't think that second course of action would end the way I wanted it to.

CHAPTER 3

IN WHICH A JACKET IS RETRIEVED

*T*his time I woke up slowly. Drifting out of a deep sleep, with the sneaking feeling I'd been dreaming but the contents of it slipped away as I became aware again. My cheek was pressed against the pillow and it felt rather like peeling it off as I woke. There was one clear thought in my head.

My new jacket.

I sat up, groaning as my head spun with lightness. I was unpleasantly damp and I had apparently torn my shirt off as I slept to counteract the heat.

Should have opened a window before I passed out...

I rubbed the bridge of my nose. I had commissioned a fine peacock feather blue jacket and waistcoat from the best tailor in town. I had been supposed to go and pick it up yesterday but with the choosing what to wear to the Hellfire Club and all, I'd been too busy. I hadn't done it, thinking I had plenty of time.

But if we were leaving Jamaica tonight, sailing at... seven? Nine? Whatever time Oliver had said? That time was all gone.

I'd already paid for the blasted jacket. I might as well enjoy it.

I pulled myself upright, found a carafe of water thoughtfully placed beside my bed by someone kind, and drained it. I could feel the cool liquid flooding my gullet, sweet and good.

Next, the chamber pot, and emptying my bladder of its rather insistent burden. Then I found a fresh shirt and pulled it over my shoulders.

I winced as the fabric hit the still oddly sensitive skin of my back.

Someone must've given me a good thrashing last night with a whip or a cane. Wish I could remember who...or what had happened afterwards.

I laced my shirt looser than normal to give my back a break, ran my fingers through my hair in lieu of a proper brush and comb, which would take time I could ill afford. I grabbed the nearest footwear I could see - a pair of sturdy but not entirely ugly boots, and stuffed my coin purse into my pocket. I'd left it at home the night before, knowing full well the kinds of people who might prey on rich idiots such as myself when the wine was flowing.

Well, wine and opium and whatever else had been going.

I decided to try and interrogate my memory later, once my jacket was in my possession and I could relax a little.

Quite accustomed to sneaking around, I could be rather silent in the hallways when I chose to. I chose to then. I remembered with some shame how pathetically rude I'd been with Oliver, and I didn't wish him to scold me or worse, go for another round of 'let's talk about how disappointing Cedric's behaviour is'. I hated that game.

But all the same, I wanted to sneak a look at him. My patheticness was really all down to the ridiculous crush I'd nursed for him since Father first hired him. There he'd been, all scrubbed and clean in a brand new suit, fresh faced and ready to imbue me with a thrill for learning and, I presumed, a better moral compass than the one I had apparently been born with.

We'd become fast friends on the interminable voyage from

London, and he hadn't been too awful about the whole lessons and tutelage thing.

I crept towards his door and was gratified to find it open. Inside, I could see Oliver moving about, picking up shirts and folding them. I positioned myself in the shadow of the door and allowed myself to just stare at him.

He wasn't much taller than I, perhaps a little more muscular. He'd mentioned some dock-work to pay for his rooms as he studied in university once or twice. His shirts fit him very well, especially since I'd started paying for my tailor to make his clothing (and possibly had hinted to the tailor that his clothes could be on the tighter side). I liked his fondness for rolling his sleeves up and displaying the soft downy hairs on his forearms.

It wasn't purely a physical attraction, mind you. I loved how he saw who I was clearly, but he still could smile at me, or be patient, or try to make things easier. Kind. He had an unfailing kindness that I found hard to understand.

He started whistling as he worked, some tune from a sea shanty we'd heard on the trip over, all those months ago.

All right, I'm definitely stalling now. I should get going.

But I lingered a few moments longer, and watched as he bent to place some shirts into his chest, then added a layer of tissue paper. His trousers tightened with the movement and I thought of several unspeakable things I could do to him and his arse.

And then he straightened and I thought about how perfect a composition he'd make, with the soft island light diffusing through the mesh curtains and bringing out the gold in his hair.

Beautiful.

I hurried down the stairs and out the front door. Ionie was beating a carpet that usually sat in the living room. I expected the house would be cleaned and leased to someone else within a day.

"Master Cedric," she called as I rushed past her. "Oliver was most insistent on the time of your departure. Do you wish for me to continue to pack your things?"

"No need," I said. "I'll be back in the shake of dancing girl's arse."

Ionie made a scoffing noise, but I was quite pleased with that turn of phrase, so I was smiling at my own puerile humour as I made my way through the city to the tailor's, adjusting my shirt collar as I went.

Judging by the position of the sun, I had slept a few hours, and the rest had done me some good. The fresh air cleared my mind more thoroughly. Or possibly it had been the water I'd swallowed?

At any rate, the sunlight wasn't as painful on my eyes, and my limbs had ceased aching. I felt halfway human again. There was even the idea for a painting tugging at the back of my head.

It would be Ionie on the front porch, beating a rug with a twisted wicker carpet beater - the colours of the rug reflected in the flowers that lined the garden path, the sunlight reflecting on the windows...

It could be quite charming. Except, of course, that I wouldn't get the chance to paint it from life if I had to sail for grey old England tonight.

I wondered if I would be able to recall it from memory in a manner satisfactory enough to capture the beauty. It didn't matter, either way.

The tailor's wasn't far from my home, so it took little time to get there. The shop was one in a row of fashion based stores, a milliner's, a cobblers, a rival tailors and then my man. His sign read "Providing the latest in European fashions" and his name was painted beneath: Victor Howard Phillips, est. 1690.

As I let myself in, the bell over the door rang and my heart tugged sadly, thinking that I wouldn't hear it again after this visit. I had grown rather fond of the old man and his clever ways with needle and thread.

"Good afternoon, Master Cedric," Mister Phillips said, looking up from the shirt he was sewing. His eyes widened as if in surprise.

Perhaps he hadn't expected me for a few more days? "Good afternoon, Mister Phillips," I said. It was easy to be polite and proper with people I respected. "I do hope you're well."

"Quite well, thank you. You must be here for your jacket. Let me fetch it for you."

"Indeed." I gave him my most charming smile, then let it drop. "I shall have to thank you for all your service to me. I shall miss you, indeed."

"Miss me?" He had moved to the back of the store and was rifling through a rack of clothing, half of it pre-made and waiting for a purchaser, but he had custom made pieces in there as well. I did sometimes wonder why he didn't have a better organisational system, but perhaps he was of the type of creative mind that doesn't lend to such passé matters.

"I come with sad tidings." I allowed the genuine regret I felt leak into my voice. "My father has insisted on my swift return to England, and my dear tutor saw fit to obey him instantly. If it had been down to me, I would have pretended to not have received the letter, or at least booked passage on a ship in several weeks."

Mister Phillips turned back to me, the waistcoat and jacket clutched tightly in his hands. "Beg your pardon, Master Cedric, are you leaving Kingston?"

"Yes, that's the general idea. Not particularly happy about it myself, but well, when pater calls, and so on." I held my hand out for the clothing. "It's all paid for, isn't it?"

"Yes," Mr Phillips said. "Oh, uh, well perhaps I should just check that the fit is correct." He held the jacket back out of my reach.

"There's no need for that," I said. I was starting to get slightly irritated by this point. "We've had fittings for the thing, and besides you have my measurements on file. It's hardly as if you don't know what size clothes I wear. I really should be going, I have my paints to pack up."

I could see Mr Phillips' jaw working, his eyes were wide and it seemed as if he were trying to think of some reason to withhold the jacket. I cleared my throat.

"I really must insist."

His shoulders slumped and his face brightened. "Yes, of course, sorry, just... the shock of the news." He laid the waistcoat and jacket out on the countertop then began to fold them, wrapping each piece in tissue paper before bundling them in brown paper and tying the whole thing up with string.

My irritation softened. "I'm truly sorry I won't be able to visit any more, I've very much enjoyed your creations."

He handed me the package and gave me a wide smile that didn't reach his eyes. "Pleasure doing business with you. Best of luck sailing out."

First it seemed as if he wanted me to wait around in the shop, and now it feels like he wants to be rid of me as soon as possible. What strange behaviour, he's usually so very, painfully ordinary.

Whatever the reason for his actions, I was happy to take my leave of him. Not that I was truly in any hurry to get back to packing my things. If this was to be my last day in Kingston then I wished to at least visit the local tavern and have a drink.

The King's Court was down by the wharves, and thus often delightfully full of bored sailors and privateers. It was a little rougher than the kind of place a person like me was strictly *supposed* to frequent but I'd never let that stop me before.

I made my way through the street market, with all its strange wares, delicious smells and hot fresh food.

I didn't often pay the market much mind, aside from to check if anyone had brought any interesting paints from far off lands. I was scanning the stalls for just such a person, when I heard a couple of voices shouting. It wasn't entirely unheard of for fights to break out. The criminal element liked to stay quiet while the Navy was around - and the Naval men usually waited until night had fallen to get rowdy.

A witch waved at me, she had an interesting copper sheen to her skin, and her dress was of fine Indian silk. She had a selection of crystals, oddly painted cards and woven strings - charms against evil, charms against drowning. I tried to pretend that I hadn't seen her but she waved again.

"You there, boy, come here, I have something you need."

I sighed, tucked the paper parcel under my left arm and approached her stall. "I'm sure you say that to everyone who passes," I said, trying to keep my tone light so she didn't curse me.

She narrowed her eyes. "Watch your tongue, boy. And watch your back." She had something in her hand, and I tilted my head to the side, trying to make out what it was. "It's not too late yet," she said. "But it soon will be, go on take this."

"What have you got for me, there? And what will it cost?"

"Two silver florins and a kind word," she said.

I almost told her it was too much but it didn't pay to be smart with a witch. Curses and hexes were real, after all. I bit my tongue and pulled out the coins, offering them to her from an open palm. "I'm sorry for joking earlier," I said, as politely as I could manage. "Thank you for your concern, I should love to take the charm you recommend."

"Hm, well. That's a bit better." She took the coins and placed a charm in my hand. It was a thumbnail sized, oddly heavy brass idol, perhaps a god or goddess from her homeland, it was bound with thread and three crystals held against its back. "Keep it on your person, boy. It might save your life."

I slipped it into my trouser pocket. "Thank you, what does it do?"

"If I told you, you wouldn't believe me," she said. "It'll protect your dreams, maybe think of it like that."

"Sure, thank you."

"Hurry on, now," she said. "Never seen a boy with more chasing after him than you."

Chasing after me?

I glanced over my shoulder as I walked away, thinking the old bat must've been delusional. No one was chasing me.

Well, that's what I thought until a group of men jumped me in an alleyway.

CHAPTER 4

IN WHICH CEDRIC IS KIDNAPPED

I took the side alley to get to The King's Court, a thing I'd done dozens of times, if not hundreds, with no incident.

I could hear footsteps, which wasn't anything unusual, it was a busy part of town.

Then a man stood in front of me, and when I tried to step around him, he barred my way. I had been trying to hurry past, but the man forced me to stop. I looked up at him with a huff of annoyance.

He was a tall man, and had the kind of face that told you either not to mess with him, or to definitely mess with him if you wanted a beating. My heart could go either way depending on the day, but in this case I'd rather have avoided him.

His hair was deep brown, with red highlights in the afternoon sun, and his skin was the colour of oak leaves in Autumn, a deep, rich ochre with orange undertones. The kind of colour I'd struggle to reproduce in oils, although if I could...

"Cedric Hale-Harrington?" he grunted.

Cold water pooled in my stomach and I swallowed. "Uh, no, never heard of him," I said, on instinct.

"Yeah, that's him," another man said from behind me. I

didn't dare look away from the man in front of me, but my hand strayed to my hip. My hip, where I'd failed to strap on a sword or any kind of protection. Lulled into a sense of security simply because nothing like this had ever happened to me before.

What a complete fool I am.

"Aye, fits the description," a third man said, moving uncomfortably close on my right hand side. I looked down in time to see his hand reaching for my arm, and I darted out of his way. "Fine clothes, short dark hair, grey eyes, no sense of self-preservation."

Ow, all right, that description might be accurate but it hurt to have it said out loud and by a total stranger.

"If you don't mind," I said. "I'll be on my way."

"No, I don't think you will," the first man said. He drew a long, wicked looking cutlass and raised it towards my throat. I tried to back away but was caught by hands on my shoulders. I looked to see who had me and saw a truly frightening man with pale, almost grey skin, and long straight, black hair. His fingers held me tight.

"What is this? Am I being press ganged? Because I'll have you know my father is a member of the British parliament."

"Yes, you see, it is him. I told you."

"Fine, Marco, I'll give you a gold coin. Let's get him onto the ship first."

I struggled against the strange man's grasp. My paper package dropped to the ground. "Fuck, my jacket. Let me go, I say!"

"Sorry, sweetheart," the one called Marco said. "Not this time."

He held his cutlass to my throat and I went still. "Now if you agree to come quietly, this will be quite straightforward," the man behind me said. His voice was deep, almost seeming to vibrate.

Quiet, right. I don't have to do that at all.

I took a breath, raised my voice and started to yell. "Help! Someone help me!"

That's when I felt something hard and solid connect with the back of my head.

I had no way of knowing how much later it was when I woke up.

My head ached - again - but this time it was a dull ache at the back of my skull, rather than the throbbing ache of too much wine.

I groaned, tried to stretch and ease the ache in my limbs, only to find my movement severely hindered.

Tied up? Oh, now that is interesting... I squirmed a little and felt the rope cut into my wrists. *Just like that time with the not-nearly-so-proper Lady Evangeline. That was a fun night.*

A small moan escaped me before I realised I definitely wasn't in that kind of situation.

I opened my eyes to find only darkness. My mind ticked like a clock, trying to work out what was happening.

Men accosting me in an alleyway.

Men who knew my name and who I was.

A blow to the back of the head, which I could still feel.

Ropes and a blindfold.

Oh right. Kidnapped. I wonder who by? The men in the alley didn't look familiar.

And now that I was working things out, I realised there was a motion I was feeling. Motion that was sickeningly familiar. I was on a ship at sea.

"Fuck," I said.

My first thought was of Oliver. He'd miss me. Or I'd miss him. It'd be up to him to explain what had happened to my parents, the poor thing. I didn't want to worry him... or well, worry him any more than I already did on a daily basis.

Poor Oliver. I'd miss him, horribly. I wondered how long it'd be before I could get back to him.

I tried to get into a sitting position - tricky with my legs bound as well as my arms, which were pinioned behind my back so tightly I could barely move them. I bit down another moan. It really wasn't the time to think about being bound for pleasure. I had to focus.

I managed to get myself upright, but there was nothing to lean against. I was part way through tossing my head side to side to see if I could dislodge the blindfold when I heard heavy footsteps - boot heels on a wooden deck, and the sound of a lock being opened.

"Fuck," I said again.

"Indeed," a voice said. I couldn't tell for sure if it was one of the men from the street, so I kept my mouth shut.

The footsteps came closer, and someone pushed the blindfold down my face so it settled around my neck.

I blinked a couple of times and looked up into the eyes of my captor.

Handsome.

Weirdly, I did sort of recognise him. I couldn't pick from where, though. He was tall, his eyes were a blazingly bright hazel colour, his stare was intense. His hair was a sandy blond colour, and he was dressed all in black. Leather pants, a black shirt and crossed bandoliers loaded with bullets as well as a sword and pistol at his hips.

"Pirate," I said, before I could stop myself. Sometimes my mouth just said things without my mind's intervention.

His mouth tugged up at the side a little and his eyes crinkled. *Handsome,* I thought again.

"Very astute, Mister Hale-Harrington. I hope you're comfortable."

That had to be a jibe, but I couldn't help myself writhing in order to feel the way the ropes cut into my skin, because it was hot, and it made my cock throb in a pleasant way. I managed to swallow an out loud response this time though, because it seemed like it wasn't the time to beg him to fuck me. It seemed as if he had more to say before I did that.

"Do you recognise me?" he asked.

"I thought I did, but I couldn't place you, I'm sorry," I said. My voice was a little hoarse, it turned out, when I had to string more than one word together.

"Have you heard of the Devil's Whore?" he asked.

I blinked. Of course I had. Everyone had. The Devil's Whore was one of the most feared pirate ships on the seven seas. The captain was nicknamed Lucifer. The captain, who always wore black and had eyes that were said to pierce the soul of his many victims.

I felt a thrill of fear, which, because I'm an idiot who had no sense of self-preservation and clearly somewhat disturbed, sent another pleasurable throb into my cock.

"Yes," I said, belatedly. I swallowed the arousal down and cleared my throat. "Are you Lucifer? Was I kidnapped by the most feared pirate on the seas since Bloody Tate?"

He smiled wickedly, smug and self-satisfied. "Indeed."

"That's fantastic," I said. I tried to sit up straighter, tried to get closer to him somehow.

"Fantastic?" He frowned, his eyebrows drew together. "In what way?"

He spoke well, with the hint of a London accent.

"It's sexy as Hell," I said. "Are you kidding me? I've literally imagined this as I lay in bed alone and stroked myself off. I mean, I'd never seen you but I imagined you were handsome... I had no idea how handsome you'd be."

He didn't respond. His eyebrows were drawn closely together. He opened his mouth and then closed it again. Folded his arms. Then tipped his head to the side.

"You are not what I imagined either, it's safe to say."

I hoped that meant I was more handsome than he thought I'd be. Probably he just hadn't expected me to be so crude and sexually magnetic.

"Right, so, I'm ready," I said, nodding a little.

"Ready for what, exactly?" he asked, faintly.

"Do me," I said.

"I'm sorry, what?"

"I can probably roll over, but you'll have to remove my trousers. I'm ready, you should fuck me." I looked him in the eyes and tried to give him my most alluring smile. I suspected the effect of it was lessened by the blindfold, which was brushing the bottom of my chin but I had to work with what I had.

He coughed and shook his head. "No, that's not... No. That won't happen."

"It won't?" Disappointment stabbed in my stomach and I bit my lip. "Why not?"

"You're my prisoner, it's not ethical."

"You're a pirate," I said. I shifted side to side and shook my head. "I hardly think problems of ethics would bother you. Where did you even learn about ethics, for Heaven's sake. I can't imagine you with a tutor."

"We're not having this conversation," Lucifer said. "I'm ransoming you for a lot of money from your parents, and then we're parting ways. That's how it's going to be." He crouched in front of me and looked me in the eyes.

"But what if I don't want to -"

I didn't get to complete my sentence, because he took the blindfold and slipped it up and into my mouth. He reached his muscular arms around me and tied the back of the blindfold - now a gag - extra tight.

Fuck if that didn't make me even hotter. He was so close. I could smell him, a soft scent of leather and rum. Maybe an undertone of vanilla? Who was this man?

"I'll send someone later to feed you, and show you to the chamber pot. If you behave we can untie you, but you'll remain locked in this room, understand?"

He sat back, his hands moving to his thighs, and I breathed out slowly, wishing he'd have kissed me over the gag. My kidnapping fantasies were *not* coming true in the ways I'd wanted.

I nodded, feeling sad, now.

He ruffled my hair - which seemed at least a little more intimate than his words had been - and left the room, locking the door behind him.

How quickly I'd forgotten about Oliver and lusted after Lucifer. How fickle and inconstant my foolish heart was. Or maybe it wasn't my heart, but something lower down...

The door didn't open again for what felt like a very long time.

CHAPTER 5

IN WHICH CAPTAIN LUCIFER YEARNS

*T*hat night, Gabriel didn't dare to return to the cabin they had Cedric Hale-Harrington locked in. Instead he sent Marco, who had been one of the men to take him from the streets of Kingston. Marco was, at heart, a sweet man and very kind, but he had a very good scary visage, and he had a knack for looking frightening when it was needed.

He'd sent Marco to untie the boy. It didn't bear to think too much about how beautiful Cedric had looked, bound at his feet, his trousers straining over the telltale bulge between his legs. His cheeks flushed and his eyes yearning...

Gabriel shook his head. *No, it wasn't right to think about that at all.*

So, Marco had gone to untie the boy and give him some dinner and a flask of water. Showed him the chamber pot.

Gabriel wasn't thinking about it at all. Especially not the way Cedric's lips had looked with the gag between them. He certainly hadn't thought about him as he'd fallen asleep in his lush captain's cabin, stripped of the black clothes that marked him as Lucifer. He certainly hadn't stroked himself...

It was the next day, and Gabriel hadn't been thinking of Cedric much at all. Or rather, he'd told himself he hadn't been thinking about him, when really his thoughts continued to return to the thought of them on his ship, willing and wanting,

Gabriel looked at the map spread out between himself and his quartermaster, Dante. Quartermaster and First Mate. Dante fulfilled both roles, really. It had been a full night and half a day since they'd taken Cedric, and thanks to the lightness of the ship, they'd been able to slip out of Kingston harbour well before the tides shifted enough to allow the Naval ship to pursue.

"So far, so good," he said.

Dante grunted, unimpressed. Gabriel looked up at him with one eyebrow raised.

"It's hardly soon enough for optimism," Dante said. "We may have avoided the Trinity Royal, but sooner or later word will get out that we took the boy from the streets of Kingston. The Navy will send out their magical alerts and every ship in the fleet will be looking for the Devil's Whore."

Gabriel sighed in a long suffering sort of way. "We evaded any notice on land, through whatever luck Marco was able to manage, and we have him contained." He resisted the urge to add 'for now', but only barely. "The Navy may have seen our ship, but they can never catch us. The Whore's the fastest ship on the Caribbean, that's partially why I named her that."

"I have a bad feeling, and not only because every time we talk about the boy, your cheeks flush. What happened between the two of you?"

If it had been any other ship perhaps the Quartermaster wouldn't speak so freely with the Captain, challenging him in such a manner. But Gabriel had known Dante for years, and the two had concocted the scheme of the pirate ship together.

Gabriel trusted Dante with his life, and more than that, the lives of all those aboard the Devil's Whore. Many would not.

Gabriel sighed and took a seat on his intentionally throne-like favourite chair. "He asked me to fuck him. Practically demanded it."

Dante sputtered out a surprised laugh. "I beg your pardon."

"Indeed," Gabriel said. "He said being kidnapped was... something he had dreamed of. You know, carnally."

Gabriel's voice became more posh the more uncomfortable he was. In that moment, he betrayed his upper class London education even more than usual.

"Well then," Dante said. "Why not indulge him? You're clearly interested, and he practically demanded it, you said."

"It's not right," Gabriel insisted. He rubbed his hand over his forehead, massaged his temples and then looked up at Dante with a measure of desperation. "He's our prisoner, I'd be taking advantage."

Dante sniffed, shrugged one shoulder and waved a hand dismissively. "He asked for it."

Gabriel shook his head. "No, I cannot-"

There was a knock on the door and Gabriel raised his voice. "Come in!"

Marco entered, looking somewhat shamefaced. "Captain, begging your pardon."

"What is it, Marco? And there's no need for such formality, you know that."

Marco pushed his shoulder length brown hair behind his ears. "Sorry, Cap. The only thing is, uh, the prisoner. Cedric."

Dante smiled, which wasn't something he did a lot, and it was always vaguely threatening when he did. "What about him?"

"Well, he keeps on asking about you," Marco said. His grey blue eyes shining with ill-concealed amusement, although he did still have an air of nervousness about him. Gabriel wasn't sure if it was because he was interrupting their conversation, or because he had news he didn't want to share.

Dante sniggered. It was a deep and sort of cruel sound. "This is what happens when you target someone known to frequent the Hellfire Club, that's all I'll say on the matter." Dante said.

"Please let that be true," Gabriel said, rolling his eyes up to Heaven.

"Only, I sent Kaito in with his breakfast and he made him uncomfortable. The way he was asking about you, Kaito doesn't want to go back in there. And I went in at lunch and it was more of the same. Perhaps he might, uh, settle down somewhat, if he were allowed to leave the room? Just for a walk around? Or perhaps you could go back in there Captain, set the record straight as it were."

Marco smiled then, obviously relieved to have said his piece, and now free to enjoy Gabriel's discomfort.

"Thank you, Marco, he shan't be allowed out, it's far too soon. And I'll go and see him but not until tomorrow. Leave him alone, perhaps some time on his own will settle his spirits and calm him down."

Even as he said it, Gabriel wasn't sure he believed it. Men like that, who were so hot blooded and enthusiastic about the carnal arts? That passion didn't usually die overnight.

He waited until Marco had left and closed the door before leaning forward and resting his head in his hands.

What the fuck have I gotten myself into this time?

Dante put a hand on his shoulder in what would have been a comforting gesture, if Dante's hands weren't cold as the grave. "There, there, Captain," Dante said, a trickle of amused irony in his voice. "So far, so good, that's what you said, wasn't it?"

"Oh, do shut up."

CHAPTER 6

IN WHICH THERE IS AN INCIDENT WITH THE QUARTERMASTER

*B*eing kidnapped wasn't nearly as exciting as I'd dreamed it would be. Obviously it had started out rather promising with the ropes and the gag and all, but then it had frankly become boring. Here I was, trapped on a pirate ship. *A pirate ship!* Full of handsome and mysterious, brooding and dangerous men, and not a one of them had laid so much as a finger on me.

It was incredibly disappointing.

And there was absolutely nothing to do in the confounded room they had me locked up in. I had a chamber pot, a bed, well, more like a hard cot, and a small scrap of a blanket. Barely enough to cover me when I finally gave in to the boredom and slept.

I had the tiniest of portholes to look out of, and it was grimy and I could barely see the ocean. There was no land in sight - of course - and the vague rolling waves were terribly boring.

If only I could get out onto the deck and see the sights for real.

If only I could paint the ship, the mast standing tall against the clear blue sky…

Or even better, convince the gorgeous Captain Lucifer to show me his mast, standing tall...

The sound of the key in the door woke me up from the fitful slumber I had managed on the bed. I sat up, heart soaring - company! And possibly it would be Captain Lucifer!

It was Marco again. One of the ruffians who'd kidnapped me.

To be honest, he wasn't at all bad looking. He had one of those dimples in his chin, and a fine head of dark brown hair. A hint of chest hair peeked out from the open collar of his shirt.

If I hadn't seen Captain Lucifer, perhaps I'd have been more excited to see Marco. But as it was I sighed and flopped back on the bed.

"You again. When will the charming captain be returning, may I ask?"

Marco put a new bottle of water down beside the bed and picked up the empty one. "As long as you keep asking about him, he won't."

"Well, that's spectacularly unfair."

Marco didn't respond, and I had the sudden fear he was just going to turn and walk out again and I couldn't bear to be left alone again so soon. "Wait, please," I said.

He must have heard the desperation in my voice, because he did wait. "Yes?"

"I'm so bored in here, please won't you stay and talk to me at least a little?"

I swung my legs over the edge of the bed and gave him a pleading look. It was a good look, I'd used it to excellent effect on some of my previous lovers when they hadn't been inclined to give me my way.

Marco sighed and tilted his head at me. "Talk? About what? I have work I need to do, or the Captain'll have my hide."

I saw a little telltale spark of something in his eyes, some interest, yes, but perhaps humour? He wasn't entirely telling the truth about what the Captain would or would not do?

"Well, if you have work to do, I won't keep you," I said. I got up off the bed and walked towards him. "But perhaps, if you were to conveniently forget to the lock the door, I could, you know, take a look around?"

Marco folded his arms, the empty bottle sticking out from under his elbow. "Absolutely not."

I looked down at the ground and then back up at him. "I'd not cause any trouble. I just want to perhaps find a book to read or something to do? A pack of cards? I'm so utterly bored locked up in this room. There's nothing to do."

Marco shook his head. "No."

"How would you like it?" I gestured around, warming to the topic, for although Marco had said no, he hadn't left the room, he was staying to listen. Something in the tug at the corner of his mouth told me he wasn't as cruel as he was pretending to be. I blundered on. "Just me, the four walls, a bed and a chamber pot, I'm stifled in here. Please, Marco? You can watch me if you like, I just need a little walk and then I'll come back to the room, as you please."

He looked at the door and then back at me, chewing his lower lip. I was getting through to him. I moved closer.

"How would you like it, being cooped up all day and night?"

That was it, just the push I needed. Marco sighed.

"All right, just for a few minutes." He stepped back, held the door open and let me walk out. "If anyone asks, you slipped past me and I'm chasing you down. Three minutes."

"Five," I said, already smiling. I was, naturally, being held in the belly of the ship. Not up off the deck itself, and although I longed to see the sunlight I wasn't foolish enough to head up onto the deck and expose myself.

Maybe next time.

So I went to the next door along, which was standing ajar and nosed my way inside.

There was a man in there, the scary man with the iron grip who'd held onto my arm during the kidnapping. I wondered if it was his rope work I'd enjoyed...

I should probably avoid other people. I should. But I didn't get the best look at him, he could be handsome, too...

I cleared my throat and walked into the room.

He turned instantly, his long, thick black hair swirling around his shoulders. His eyes seemed to reflect what little light I'd let in from the hallway, almost catlike.

His cheekbones looked like they'd cut my finger if I touched them. His jaw was on the slim side, aiming downwards to his pointed chin.

"The prisoner. What are you doing in here?"

His voice had a pleasant timbre to it, deep but soft. As if he were holding something back, speaking gently on purpose.

I walked straight up to him, a little entranced. "I sneaked past Marco," I lied.

He frowned at me. I saw his nostrils flare a little. I became aware of how my heart was pounding and how no one had touched or kissed me in what was it? Days? How long had I been on this ship again? It was hard to tell when I kept falling asleep out of pure boredom.

"You ought to get back to your room," he said. He straightened his posture as I got closer. He had a few inches on me, and his frame was slender, but I could see the muscles under his shirt. He had a sword at his hip, slimmer than the one the captain carried.

"You ought to kiss me," I said. And actually, that time, I hadn't quite meant to be so forward. I had meant to ask his name.

"I'm sorry, what was that?" His lip curled in a sneer. "I thought you'd been begging the captain to fuck you."

"Oh, you know about that?" I felt my cheeks heat a little. Something about this man was flustering me. My brain was miscommunicating with my mouth, or perhaps there was some animal instinct driving me, something more than just lust, because I felt a little nervous as well. As if I were in the room with a dangerous predator.

"Cedric!" Marco called. "Get back here!"

I ignored Marco's cry. I found myself curiously unable to break eye contact with the predator. I raised a trembling hand to touch the black haired man's chest. His skin felt oddly cool through the thin cotton of his shirt. He had an amulet of some kind hanging from a chain - a witch's charm, perhaps?

His jaw clenched. "Don't touch me," he hissed through his teeth.

I flattened my palm on his chest, feeling the heat from my hand leech into him. "I want to touch you," I said, although a part of me was also insisting I flee.

In the back of my head I heard something that almost sounded like Oliver's voice, telling me to listen to Marco and do as he said or there'd be consequences.

I ignored it all and lost myself in the deep green eyes of the cold man. "Move away from me, now," he said. It was an order. If he'd ordered me to my knees I'd have done it. But move away? I didn't want to do that at all.

"Are you afraid?" I asked. I leaned in closer, my heart pounding, my fingers curling to dig into his chest a little, showing him how much I wanted him.

He closed his hand around my wrist and opened his mouth. My gaze dropped then, drawn to his teeth. There was something about them. Something that the cautious and seldom heeded part of my mind insisted I look at.

"Dante! Stop that this instant!"

The black haired man stepped back from me quickly, letting go of my hand. I turned to see Captain Lucifer in the doorway.

His shirt hung half open and he was barefoot, a more casual version of the impressive pirate.

No less attractive, of course.

"Captain, I wouldn't have done-"

"Obviously you wouldn't have," Lucifer strode into the room and grasped me by the bicep, pulling me behind him with such force I stumbled, he held me up with his grip. "Because you know that Cedric here is worth an awful lot of coin, and if we damage him in any way then he will be worth a lot less."

Damage me?

Dante, the black haired man, had moved back as far as he could, pressing himself to the wall of the ship, one hand up over his mouth. He nodded. "Of course, Captain."

Lucifer huffed, yanked me further back and led me from the room.

"Sorry, Captain," Marco said, from further up the hallway. "He slipped past me."

"It's nothing," Lucifer said. "I've obviously got to keep a closer eye on our idiotic hostage."

"I beg your pardon," I said, outraged. "I am not idiotic! I am spirited and delightful!"

"Shut up." Lucifer led the way, hauling me behind him. We went past the room I'd been locked in and up the stairs to the deck.

Daylight! Blessed, wonderful daylight!

I inhaled the sea air and felt it fill my lungs. The sky was cerulean and there were only the smallest, fluffiest of white clouds up there.

I stumbled over my feet as Lucifer yanked me through a door and into what had to be his own cabin. The only one that opened out onto the main deck. He threw me bodily inside and I stumbled and fell flat on my face. I rolled over, hoping that there was more coming, some kind of punishment for having broken the rules. Some painful and pleasurable punishment.

"Sit down and shut up. I'll deal with you later," he growled. Actually growled.

He slammed the door shut and locked it from the outside.

I glanced around the room. It was quite lush, with books and things. Not to mention a bed that actually looked comfortable. He hadn't told me *where* to sit down and shut up, therefore it was up to me to decide.

I dusted off my trousers and picked myself up off the floor. I might have a bruise on my shoulder from being thrown, but I could forgive the captain that. I had no way of knowing how long it'd be before he returned, so I settled on the bed.

What had happened with Dante? And why was Lucifer so angry about it? It had seemed like more than just 'you got out of your room'. I did hope he wasn't punishing Marco.

With nothing to do but wait, I let myself ponder what might happen when the captain returned.

CHAPTER 7

IN WHICH CAPTAIN LUCIFER DEALS WITH
VARIOUS POOR DECISIONS

*G*abriel locked the door to his cabin - something he did
so rarely he half worried the lock wouldn't hold - and
then stormed back down into the hold to talk to Dante.
Or yell at him.

Dante was much where Gabriel had left him. He had moved
so he was sitting cross legged on the floor, his eyes closed.
Meditating or mastering his urges or something like that.

He opened his eyes when Gabriel stomped in and stopped in
front of him, arms folded.

"Well?"

"What do you expect me to say?" Dante asked, testily.

"I thought you'd fed at Kingston," Gabriel said. "How are we
supposed to keep the boy safe if you can't control your hunger?"

"I did. I'm not hungry, not like that," Dante got to his feet and
squared his shoulders. This was gearing up to be a fight and he
wanted to look Gabriel in the eye.

"Well, it certainly looked like you were about to feed off him
when I walked in," Gabriel growled.

"He practically thrust his neck in my mouth," Dante said. "I
can't be held responsible. The boy is incorrigible, liable to fuck
anything that moves as far as I can tell."

Gabriel snorted and raised an eyebrow. "I don't care if he opens a vein in front of you, you're not to feed off him. We return him to his family with scars on him, they'll use all their political power to hunt us down."

"I know," Dante snapped. "I'm aware."

"So get your blasted hunger under control."

Dante shoved his hands deep into his pockets, hunched his shoulders and looked down. When he spoke his voice was soft and more compliant. "Yes, Captain."

"I'll keep him in my cabin from now on," Gabriel said. "So you shouldn't see him again anyway, certainly not alone."

Dante opened his mouth and then closed it without saying a word. Gabriel couldn't stand when his friend and most trusted crew mate didn't speak his mind, so although he was still annoyed, he prompted him.

"Well? What do you want to say?"

"There is something about him," Dante said, his voice even quieter than it had been. "Something alluring."

"Because he was trying to fuck you," Gabriel said. "And he's handsome. Handsome and willing is a deadly combination."

"It felt like more than that somehow," Dante said, almost wistfully. Then he shook his head. "Forget it. I understand, I'll keep my distance. But, perhaps don't be too hard on Marco? We've both seen, felt perhaps, the effect the boy can have."

Gabriel nodded. "I thought I'd just tell him to have a swim, think about what he's done."

Dante nodded. "A fine idea."

"And if you get hungry before we make port again, for God's sake say something to me, all right?"

Dante rolled his eyes and nodded. "Yes, Captain, I'll tell you. But it's highly unlikely to happen."

"See that it doesn't."

. . .

Gabriel went back up onto the deck, his shoulders a little less tense than they had been. Dante's condition didn't often complicate matters, but it did need to be taken into account sometimes.

Marco was lingering near the main mast, shame-faced and looking downtrodden.

In all honesty, Gabriel agreed with Dante - the boy was charismatic and there was something compelling about him. He didn't really blame Marco for somehow letting him free. But he couldn't commiserate or say he understood either. He was the Captain, and the rest of the crew had to see that there were consequences.

"Marco," he said, sharply. A little louder than necessary, so the others would hear. "Have you anything to say for yourself?"

"No, Cap," Marco said. He looked up, grimacing, expecting Gabriel to shout perhaps, or order the lash. Well, he was in luck today.

"Good. You're on dinner clean up for a week," Gabriel said. "And go for a swim until sundown."

It was a punishment he couldn't possibly give anyone else on the ship. But Marco nodded, knowing that as punishments went, it was a relatively kind one.

"Yes, Captain."

"Think about what would have happened if the boy had jumped overboard, or hurt himself, or worse, got hold of a weapon and hurt one of us."

"Yes, Captain." Marco dropped his eyes again and looked at his feet, but there was a nervous excitement to him now, which Gabriel recognised as an eagerness to return to the ocean.

"Go on, then."

Marco went to the side of the ship, stripped off his shirt and his loose fitting striped trousers, revealing his somewhat stocky but well muscled and generously haired body.

He climbed up on the side of the ship then shifted into otter form. He was a sea otter, around the size of a small labrador, with a pleasing countenance. He turned and blinked at Gabriel before diving overboard into the waters of the Caribbean.

Gabriel, and much of the crew come to that, never tired of watching the transformation, and it wasn't until the telltale splash that Gabriel cleared his throat and shouted again.

"Back to work, lads!"

The general business of the ship resumed. Gabriel took the helm to distract himself for a time.

Once the watch had changed, Gabriel ate his dinner with a few of the other crew and took a plate of leftovers up to to his cabin.

He unlocked the door with the key he'd hung from a chain around his neck and let himself in, being careful to lock the door behind him again.

"I hope you're ready to be reasonable," Gabriel said. He was avoiding looking at Cedric, although he was aware he was on the bed - which was already setting an uncomfortable feeling in his stomach.

Cedric cleared his throat, and Gabriel looked up to see him, sprawled on his side on the bed, propping his head up on one hand, one leg hitched up, and utterly naked. Gabriel very nearly dropped the tray of food he was carrying - only his preparatory school training prevented it.

"I'm always reasonable," Cedric said, as innocently as you please.

CHAPTER 8

⚜

IN WHICH AN AGREEMENT IS VERY
CAREFULLY NEGOTIATED

*I*n all honesty, I was hungry. But I wanted to get this done first. I wanted to break this barrier that Captain Lucifer had put up. I didn't just want to experience sex with a real life pirate, I wanted him to see that there was absolutely no problem with it.

He didn't seem to share my perspective, but I was confident I could bring him around to my way of thinking.

He carefully set the tray of food down on his desk and shook his head.

"Put your clothes on, Cedric."

I didn't move, but I watched his body - his large, trim but muscular form, encased in black. His boots stood high to his knees, cutlass at his hip. His blond hair pushed back from his face, and his eyes flashing blue as the ocean outside the window. Telltale swell of a bulge in his trousers, which I let my gaze linger on before smiling up at him.

"I shan't."

"You must." He raked a hand through his hair, exasperated, and shook his head. "I'm the Captain of this ship, and I have kidnapped you. To do anything with you, anything at all is gross misuse of power. It's not a balanced exchange, do you understand? I'd be taking advantage."

"You wouldn't." I sat up now, letting my legs fall apart nice and wide. I was rewarded when Lucifer's eyes flicked down and then back up. His luscious lips parted.

He's definitely interested. He just has some kind of ethical objection.

"Sweet as it is that you - a pirate who named himself after Satan - has a code of honour, I can assure you there's no reason to be bashful with me. I've slept with ... God knows how many people, men, women, undecided. I've taken it, I've given it, I've been entangled in several at once. I can assure you I'm sober and know exactly what I'm asking for."

Lucifer folded his arms and huffed out a sigh. "Cedric."

"And if it's my Father you're worried about, you have nothing to fear there, too. I've been lying to him as long as I can remember. I'll tell him that you left me locked in the brig and that I've seen the error of my ways." I licked my lips, I could see him wavering. I swallowed, I didn't want to mess this up. "And besides, you said yourself I'll be stuck in here with you and no one else, and I get so very lonely. Please? Lucifer, listen, I'm begging you." I shuffled to the edge of the bed, braced my hands on the wooden base and looked up at him with my best 'lost puppy in need' expression.

He sighed again, turned away so I couldn't see his expression. His hand strayed down to his bulge and he seemed to rub it, or adjust himself somehow.

"Eat your dinner," he said. "I'll be back shortly." Then he left the cabin and locked the door behind him again.

Disappointing, to be sure, but it wasn't a refusal.

A flare of hope in my stomach, I crossed to the tray. No cutlery on offer, but a pretty decent cheese scone, some slices of now cold pork and a bit of gravy. I shovelled it all in greedily.

Dinner demolished, I washed my hands in a bowl of water and dried them off on a towel before settling back on the bed.

Although I hoped that Lucifer would return soon, and with an enthusiastic assent, I idly stroked my own cock while I waited for him, my other hand tucked behind my head, and dreamed of Lucifer and Dante both.

I heard the key in the lock and slowed my hand because, as disturbed as I was, I wanted him to catch me in the act. Perhaps I wanted to provoke something of a possessive reaction?

I turned my head to look at him, delighting in the surprise in his expression, and indeed, at the glimpse of the rest of the ship behind him through the open door. The idea that some other member of the crew might see simply excited me more.

"Cedric," Lucifer said, his voice now a low growl. He slammed the door shut, making me jump a little, and hastily locked the door.

"Yes?" I asked, as innocently as I could make my voice sound.

"Get your hand off yourself this instant!"

The force of anger and dominance in his tone had me obeying instantly, even as it increased my arousal and excitement.

"Yes, Captain," I murmured.

He hung up his cutlass and belt on the wall, and set aside his varied other weapons. Then he crossed to the bed. I'd let my hand fall to the side and it lay motionless on the bed beside my hip.

"Cedric, you are utterly impossible," Lucifer growled. "Tell me what you want, again. Tell me out loud."

I swallowed, the wide world opening up in front of me - something told me whatever I asked for now, I'd get it from him. His eyes pierced mine and pinned me to the bed, powerless under his aura of command but free to ask for my heart's desire.

"I want you to kiss me and fuck me and tie me up and make me suck you and have you suck me and honestly anything you're into, I want to try because you're absolutely gorgeous," I said, my worlds almost falling over each other in my hurry to say it all at once.

"Oh for fuck's sake," Lucifer breathed. "You're going to keep on doing all of these ridiculous things unless I bed you, aren't you?"

"Yes." I nodded. "I really do want you, and... And I think you want me too."

He took a breath in through his nose and let it out in one whoosh. "Yes. Tell me what you want once more."

I licked my lips. "I want you to kiss me, fuck me, and ... just a whole lot of other stuff too."

"Ask nicely, say please," he growled.

"Please, Captain Lucifer, will you please fuck me?" I felt goose pimples spring up over my arms as I spoke, I was trembling and needy and desperately wanting this to work.

In an instant he was on me, his mouth on mine, demanding and passionate.

His hands found my wrists and wrenched them up over my head, pinning me to the mattress as he settled his body on top of mine, pushing my legs apart and pressing his hardness against mine. Naked as I was, his trousers produced extra friction on me and I moaned loudly, closing my eyes and taking everything he was giving me.

He broke the kiss and looked deep into my eyes. "Be quiet," he hissed.

"I can't promise anything," I said, smiling. I squirmed under him, tugging against the hold he had on my arms and groaning again at the sensation of his weight on me.

He pressed harder against me until the groan cut off into a gasp. I leaned up a little to kiss his jaw, a tiny growth of stubble scraped my lips and I smiled against his skin, kissing my way to his ear and gently bit his earlobe.

He gathered both my wrists into one hand and pressed them down. "Stay still," he said.

Then he sat up and stripped off his shirt. Some contrary part of me wanted to touch him, to wrap myself around him and lose myself utterly in sensations, but then I didn't want to make him regret his decision. I stayed where he'd put me, watching and salivating as he went to his knees and shoved his trousers done. He reached over me and retrieved a small pot of coconut oil.

He sat on his heels and looked me over. I felt exposed, beautiful and vulnerable. I felt desired as well, which was really my favourite thing to feel in the world.

His expression was hungry, appreciative, and he took his time raking his gaze over my chest, arms, face, stomach and then down.

His hands hooked under my knees and pressed them to my chest, exposing me to him in the most intimate way.

"Hold those there," he said. I lifted my arms then, and wrapped them around my knees, holding them in place.

"Good pup," he murmured and I flushed at the praise.

He dipped his fingers into the oil and dripped it over my hole, making me jump. He grinned and started to tease at me, pushing his fingers in before I was properly relaxed. I moaned, enjoying the sharpness of the sensation, the push of his fingers against my body and feeling myself stretch.

"God, yes, just like that," I groaned.

"I'm going to gag you in a minute," Lucifer said, but he sounded more amused than annoyed, and there was a delightful rasp to his voice now.

"You can," I said. "I'm into....ohhhhh..." My moan turned into a whine as he pushed through the tight muscle and opened me up. His fingers expertly navigating my anatomy until I was shaking with need.

"Not tonight," he whispered. "Just want to feel you tonight. Now... relax, will you?"

I breathed out and tried to relax, but it was damn hard with his fingers inside me, wiggling and teasing inside me.

"That's it, nearly…" he shifted closer and withdrew his fingers, pressing the tip of his cock against me instead, slicking himself with more oil as he got into position.

"Please, for the love of God," I begged, trying to push myself against him but finding it difficult with my legs up.

"Wrong deity," he said, grinning wickedly. I opened my mouth to tell him I wasn't going to plead with Satan, but then he pressed into me and my mind was lost to words.

"Yes, more," I gasped. He thrust his hips forward with a sharp movement and stretched me open with his impressive girth. It was like being given water after a week in the desert, or having dinner after a day of fasting. "More."

He grunted and shoved his hips hard against me. "Such a wanton boy, aren't you? Begging me for it like a whore."

I lost the grip on my knees and my legs slipped down either side of his hips. The change in angle resulted in even deeper penetration and I moaned as wantonly as the whore Lucifer had called me.

I wrapped my legs around him, hooking my ankles together behind his thighs and reached up to wind my arms around his neck.

He started to thrust in earnest then, his head dipping down to bite at my jaw and throat as I hung on and took it.

"Yes, yes, more," I panted, not needing any further words at that time.

The handsome pirate captain obliged me, and pounded me soundly into the bed. He had impressive stamina, and I found myself longing for a hand on my cock, but I was enjoying holding onto Lucifer too much to let go. And I'd lost words beyond more.

My world narrowed to the feel of his glorious cock inside me and my own racing heart beat.

I was vaguely aware of Lucifer gasping and mumbling words. One of them was definitely 'Cedric' and I nearly came simply from hearing that, but I didn't dare until Lucifer had got his pleasure.

No sooner had I thought that, then I felt Lucifer's slick hand on my cock, pumping it smoothly as he shoved himself inside.

"More, please, I'm about to..." I gasped, feeling myself tense around him.

He nodded, looking me in the eyes with that intense ice blue stare. I made a broken whining sound, high and needy, and orgasmed, closing my eyes with the force of it. Lucifer plunged deep into me and filled me, moaning softly as he did so.

Blearily, I opened my eyes again, leaned up and captured his lips in a soft but sloppy kiss, trying to thank him for what he'd given me.

He kissed me back, then gently unwound my arms and legs from around him and pulled out. Both of us sighed a little as the connection was broken. Then he cleaned me with a damp cloth, extinguished the lantern and climbed into bed beside me.

I wrapped my arms around him, rested my cheek on his shoulder and fell asleep almost immediately.

CHAPTER 9

IN WHICH THERE IS SOME TRULY AWFUL PILLOW TALK

I woke up before Lucifer did, which meant I got that magical soft moment of watching him.

In truth, it wasn't a moment I often enjoyed. I usually didn't wish to linger with my lovers, the morning conversation was often annoying or needy. I didn't wish to be needed.

Except, perhaps, by Oliver? Well, that's out of the question for the moment, isn't it. Besides, it feels wrong to think of him now.

Lucifer's body was warm beside mine, his chest gently rising and falling as he slept. I let myself take in the pale gold of his skin, the way the pink blush of his cheeks highlighted the sharpness of his cheekbones. I longed to try and recreate the colour with oils. *Portrait of the pirate in repose.*

I let my eyes drop over the jaw, shadowed and in need of a shave to the planes of his chest, soft lines accentuating hard muscles.

I didn't dare touch him - it might wake him up and then my moment of quiet observation would be done. I wasn't quite ready for that.

His shoulders were broad and brawny, making me feel rather inadequate, my own soft shoulders and arms would never hold their own against him. I imagined him overpowering me and felt a flush of warmth straight down to my crotch. *Oh yes, any time.*

The sheet, which was a surprisingly fine linen, was draped across his hip, covering his cock as if arranged by Michelangelo himself. I licked my lips. Perhaps I could wake him with my mouth?

Finally, I couldn't contain myself any longer. I had to touch him. Gently as I could, I closed my fingers on the sheet and drew it down and off his hip, revealing the thatch of honey blond hair and that glorious cock, resting heavy and full with the morning.

I moved onto my knees as slowly as possible, but in an instant Lucifer woke. He must have had a knife hidden on the side of the bed because with a swift movement I could barely follow he had a blade to my throat.

"Don't move," he growled, his voice rasping with sleep.

This eventuality did little to allay the arousal I was feeling and in fact, rather ignited it. Danger was always the most fun.

"Whatever you say," I said, allowing my eyes to close with bliss as my Adam's apple brushed against the sharpness of the blade with my words.

The blade was almost instantly gone from my throat. Somewhat disappointed, I opened my eyes once more. Lucifer had pushed his body up into a sitting position, the blade held loosely in his hand. The sheet fell to the side, leaving him resplendent in the little morning light that filtered through the leaded windows.

"Cedric," he said, as if he'd forgotten who I was or what I was doing there.

"Yes, good morning, lover," I said, giving him one of my more charming smiles.

Lucifer visibly blanched, his eyes widening with something like horror. "No, you can't say that." He glanced down at his state of undress, and then mine and groaned, but not in the way I'd hoped to have him groaning. He hurriedly pulled the sheet over himself like a surprised maiden.

"Really, no need to be so shy," I said, sitting back on my heels. "I saw it all last night, and my rear still feels the lingering after effects of the pounding you gave it. I'd rather hoped for another round, actually."

Lucifer shook his head. "This was a mistake, and it cannot happen again, if I were to form any sort of-" He cut off his own sentence, which left me wondering. Had he been about to say attachment?

I didn't want any sort of attachment, did I? No, of course not. Unless...? No.

I pushed a hand through the curls that had fallen onto my forehead and sighed.

"Don't be like that again, I've told you I don't want to marry you or anything like that, it's just good fun while you've got me as a hostage."

He shook his hand. "Last night can't be taken back, but I can behave as a gentleman from now on."

I narrowed my eyes at him. "You're a pirate, you don't need to be a bloody *gentleman*."

He looked away and got up, out of bed, holding the sheet in front of him. It was rather ridiculous. He had the blade clutched in one fist and the other twisting the sheet and maintaining his modesty.

"There's the ethics of the thing," he mumbled, putting the knife down and reaching for a pair of trousers.

Ethics again. This is getting positively tiresome.

I turned away from him, giving him his precious privacy, and folded my arms. "Fine, I'll just... I'll just become very well acquainted with my right hand for the rest of this blasted captivity, shall I? Would that please you?"

I heard him snort delicately behind me. Then the sound of fabric over legs, his trousers being settled into place on his hips,

I could just about see it in my mind's eye. But I wouldn't turn and give him the satisfaction.

"No, I don't want to think about that at all, thank you very much. I had *rather* thought I was doing you a favour, keeping you from the rest of the crew, but now perhaps -"

His sentence cut off abruptly.

"That's not the first time you've stopped talking mid-sentence," I huffed. "It's hardly gentlemanly, if you must know."

He didn't reply, which was strange, so I deigned to turn my head and looked at him over my shoulder.

His expression, which had been one of mild panic previously, was now something more like aghast. His eyes had widened and his eyebrows shot up.

"What is it?" I asked, now feeling suddenly self conscious, as if he were repulsed by my body somehow. I fought the urge to grab something to cover myself with. Ridiculous.

"I didn't notice your tattoo last night," he said, quickly looking away.

"Tattoo? I don't have a tattoo," I said. "I might be wayward, but I'm not reckless. If I had a tattoo and my father found out he'd disown me."

"Uh, yes, you do have a tattoo," Lucifer said. "It's gigantic, on your back."

My blood went cold. I had felt that strange discomfort on my back when I'd woken up a few days ago...

"I don't have a tattoo," I said, although my tone was a lot less certain. "How could I have got a tattoo without knowing about it? That's preposterous."

"It's here."

To my surprise, Lucifer moved closer behind me, knelt on the bed and placed a finger on my shoulder blade. This had been what I wanted, him to touch me, but now there was little pleasure in it. His finger traced a line down and across my spine, up to my other shoulder blade and then down, sketching some huge design over my back and down to my waist. Impossibly huge.

"What? I can't possibly have a tattoo that large, what does it depict? What does it look like?"

He dropped his hand down and swallowed. "I'm not sure, it's strange, made of black lines that swirl and... perhaps it's a dragon? I don't... It gives me a peculiar feeling."

I turned to look at him, absolutely perplexed. "I don't understand."

"You really didn't know you had a tattoo?" Lucifer tilted his head to the side, peering into my eyes. I met his gaze and shook my head.

"Of course I didn't. I'm a gentleman, we don't get tattoos unless we serve in the Navy and even then, they'd be very small indeed." My back had been sore after the night at the club, that had to be the explanation. I swallowed, smiled a smile I didn't feel and tried to respond brightly. "I expect it's some kind of stupid prank the Hellfire club pulled on me."

His eyes widened again. *Damn, they're quite green this morning, fresh Spring growth on an oak tree.*

"Yes, the Hellfire Club, you were there a few nights ago. Fuck." He got up off the bed and strode to the door.

"How did you know that?"

"I tried to find you there, but they wouldn't let me in..." He opened the door, then looked back at me. "Stay there, put some clothes on your lower half. I'm getting Dante."

"You tried to find me there? What?"

He locked the door behind him. He'd left his knife on the little shelf beside the bed, but there didn't seem to be much point in my trying to arm myself with it. Lucifer could easily overpower me and Dante could probably do the same with little trouble. Besides I was on their ship, and didn't particularly want to get away...

I found my trousers and pulled them on.

CHAPTER 10

IN WHICH A TATTOO IS EXAMINED

*L*ucifer was gone long enough that I got bored and went looking through his cabin for a mirror. His face was always clean shaven, he must have a mirror somewhere about the place. I found it in the corner, in a box with a shaving kit that I recognised as being from a gentleman's clothiers in London. One of the ones I had frequented, in fact, while I'd been living there.

But they'd never serve a pirate... probably he had stolen it from someone else.

I'd investigate it more fully on another day, but for now I was too curious about this purported tattoo on my back.

Holding the mirror in my hand, I tried to angle it over my shoulder, but turning my head and getting the mirror so that it would reflect my back was blasted difficult. Finally, I managed to catch the sight of an unfamiliar black swirl on my shoulder, which was enough of a shock for me to drop the damn mirror, which promptly slid under the bed. I was down on my hands and knees, reaching my arm under to get it back when the door opened and Lucifer and Dante walked back in.

I considered abandoning my quest for the looking glass in

order to face them, but decided they'd be quite happy to enjoy the view of my arse in the air, so I took my time retrieving it.

Finally I emerged, turned and gave them both a toothy smile. "Hello lads."

Dante, who was pale at the best of times, had gone positively ghostly.

"Did you say the Hellfire club?" Dante said, in his curiously low register.

"Yes," I said, standing up. "After months of being obvious, dropping hints and parties and generally making a nuisance of myself, I finally got an invite, and they do this! An absolute outrage, is what it is."

"Turn around," Lucifer said, in that no-nonsense tone that made my knees go weak and wobbly. I turned. They both moved closer to me and I closed my eyes, imagining two pairs of hands on my body, two mouths on my skin, two...

"I believe I know what this symbol means," Dante said. "And it is not good news, at all. Captain, perhaps we could have a word separately?"

"No, I want to know," I said, turning back around. "It's my skin, isn't it? If it means anything at all, I should definitely be included in the conversation."

Lucifer and Dante exchanged a look, turned on their heels and left the room, closing the door behind them. Indignantly, I made to follow them but I was too slow, and as my hand closed on the doorknob I heard the turn of the key in the lock.

I kicked the door and then regretted it immediately, as I hadn't put any sort of footwear on and stubbed my toe rather painfully.

Feeling ignored and mistreated, I crumpled to the ground to nurse my sore toe.

I leaned against the door and silently bemoaned my pathetic state.

"...centuries ago," Dante said, his voice somewhat hushed,

but clear enough. They'd stopped outside the door to talk and miraculously I was near enough to the door to overhear them.

"But what does it mean?" *which was exactly the question I had about it as well*

"Nothing good," Dante said, darkly.

"Dante, for the love of ... just answer plainly will you? The boy didn't even know he had it. Clearly something untoward is going on here, and now it's on my ship."

There was a sigh and then a silence, and then Dante spoke again. "When I saw it last it was associated with a dangerous and bizarre religious order. A cult, really. Bad people, Gabriel, people who didn't care who they hurt to get what they wanted."

A cult? The Hellfire Club wasn't a cult, it was just a bunch of people having some fun.

Wasn't it?

"And what do they want? Or, what did they want then?"

Dante lowered his voice and I couldn't make out the words, it was a gravelly rumble of something. I pressed my ear closer against the door but I couldn't hear him.

"And you're saying now Cedric's involved?"

"It would seem so."

"And they're going to try and get him back?"

"I'd wager so."

Get me back? Wait, that meant someone was still trying to kidnap me, even though I'd already been kidnapped?

Hadn't someone said there were a lot of people after me, back in Kingston?

I shook my head and huffed out my breath. I wanted to stay on this ship, with Captain Lucifer, especially now that I'd felt his dick inside me. *Urgh, I just want it again.*

I heard the sound of the key in the door and quickly scooted back from the door, not wanting to be hit by it.

Captain Lucifer strode in and looked down on me, confusion quickly turned into consternation on his fine features.

"What were you... were you eavesdropping?"

I scrambled to my feet, incensed now. "Yes, because whatever it is that you're discussing does rather concern me, doesn't it? It's my skin on the line from this cult or whatever you said it was."

Dante walked in behind the captain and my mind processed a few more things I'd overheard.

"And what was this about you having met the awful people before? And why did you say centuries? And while I'm at it, who is *Gabriel*?"

"No, I won't put up with this." Lucifer turned and strode out the door again.

Dante lingered for the length of a breath. He gazed at me with an inscrutable look, part fear perhaps? Then he shook his head - resembling a doctor giving some terrible news to a patient with consumption.

My heart was already racing from confusion and fear, and now, with that look my fear escalated to mild panic.

"Wait, Dante, what does it mean? Please!" I tried to step towards him but he hurried out of the room as if I were cursed.

The door locked behind them and I was once again alone.

"Am I actually cursed?" I asked the empty cabin.

CHAPTER 11

IN WHICH CEDRIC CONSIDERS

The bastards were gone for two hours.

I have a mystery tattoo on my back, and Dante saw it and was horrified and no one is telling me what it is or what it means.

I'm locked in the cabin of a pirate ship and they're afraid of me?

I paced the cabin.

I tried to look at my back in the mirror again, but I pulled something in my shoulder and had to stretch it out.

Everything had been going so well. I'd been kidnapped by sexy pirates and now they were what? Afraid of me? Ready to get rid of me? At any rate they were very much not telling me what was going on.

I sprawled on the bed and sighed, wondering what the future held for me. I was relatively sure they wouldn't just toss me overboard or run me through, Lucifer had mentioned the ransom money plenty of times after all. He wanted to be paid.

My skin, scarred as it was, was still valuable for that, at least.

My fingers twitched, aching for some outlet. Wishing for a paintbrush and colours, or for someone's body to play with.

I was part way through my twentieth, or perhaps thirtieth heartfelt sigh when the door opened and in walked Captain Lucifer and Dante.

I sat up on the bed, feeling my annoyance rise up within me again. My hands formed fists and I shook my head, feeling my curls fly about my forehead.

"Well, what's going on? Are you going to tell me anything at all?"

Lucifer strode over to me, his expression thunderous. He stopped a foot from the bed, his eyes blazing. "Don't you ever speak to me like that again, *boy*."

My anger flared into arousal. Captain Lucifer was absolutely gorgeous and the aura of command he had about him was intoxicating.

I swallowed, but didn't respond. I couldn't. I feared suddenly that if I angered him further it wouldn't go well for me.

His angry aura eased a little and his shoulders relaxed.

"We have decided on a course of action," he said finally. Dante moved through the room, getting closer to the bed. He had an aura all his own, and it was no less frightening - or less attractive.

I swallowed again, my mouth was quite dry. "Yes?"

"We will return you to your family as soon as possible. We're not so far away from Jamaica, we could bring you back to your townhouse in Kingston."

My blood went cold. "But, what is the tattoo? Dante, you said you recognised it, and there was something about a cult?"

"The cult who worship one of the old ones, one of the monsters from-" Dante said, his voice rich as chocolate and even more bitter.

"That's enough!" Lucifer snapped.

My heart sped up and I heard the blood pounding in my ears. "Monsters? What does he mean?"

Lucifer shot Dante a quelling look but he stood up straight. "I think the boy has a right to know what he's become entangled in."

The two of them stared at each other. There was tension but

also a sort of understanding. They must have known each other a very long time.

"Fine," Lucifer said, finally. He stepped back, cast about for a chair and dragged it over, sprawling in it with his legs wide apart.

Dante moved a step closer. "You were tricked by a cult, the cult of the Unknowable Way. They worship an old god, a bad, powerful old god... or perhaps it's more like a demon, or a kraken from the deep. These things, they're..." he trailed off, looking past me for a moment before seeming to remember himself. "They're not to be trifled with."

"All right..." I said, slowly. The hairs at the back of my neck prickled.

"They are always trying to bring these gods into our world, and if they were to succeed, well." He shook his head. "Let us pray that they do not succeed." His eyes were hard and shiny, and he frowned, his eyebrows pulled together.

"And you know all this, because, what? You've met them before?" I glanced at Lucifer, who had pulled out one of his knives and was using the tip of it to clean under his fingernails.

Dante sat down on the bed, close enough to touch, and I felt my breath catch in my throat. That weird magnetism he had about him had me entranced all over again.

"I met them once before, many years ago," Dante said. "That's all you need to know. Turn around, show me the symbol on your back again?"

I didn't think of disagreeing with him. He was actually telling me things, and even though they were frightening things, I didn't want to break whatever spell it was making him talk. I turned away from him, watching Lucifer as Dante examined my back.

His finger, very softly, traced a shape over my back. I couldn't hide my arousal, I felt my lips part and my trousers tighten.

"The sign of the crawling chaos. This is no ordinary tattoo."

"Well, obviously," I said, despite myself. I didn't want him to stop touching me, but I couldn't resist saying that.

"Why did they put it on him?" Lucifer asked, sheathing his knife again and leaning his elbows on his knees.

Dante's hand withdrew, and I turned back towards him. "Yes, why was it me?"

Dante shrugged. "Perhaps they thought you an easy mark, or perhaps a powerful possibility. I'm sure they expected you to stay put in Jamaica, and that perhaps, no one would miss you."

I felt a sour taste in the back of my mouth. "I'd be very missed," I said. "Oliver will be missing me terribly, and after that, my parents back in London."

"Who's Oliver?" Lucifer asked.

"Gabriel, this is not the time," Dante said, and Lucifer gave him another look. It took a moment and then it dawned on me.

"Is your name really Gabriel?" I asked, my voice getting louder than I meant it to.

"Thank you, Dante, that was very helpful of you," Lucifer said, his voice dripping in irony.

I bit my lip to stop myself. I wanted to tell him how it was a beautiful name, and one that suited his angelic appearance. That was the connection as well, I realised. Lucifer was a fallen angel, and Gabriel was an archangel.

"The fact of the matter is, they marked you for a reason, Cedric. Something dark. They're going to want you back."

"Then you can't take me to Jamaica!" I said. I reached for Dante's hand and clasped it. "Please, they'll want to torture me or skin me or sacrifice me on an altar."

Dante's hand was curiously cold in mine, but he didn't pull back. Looking into his eyes I felt a sort of trust that he wouldn't hurt me. He was on my side, he wouldn't give me up to the cult. I can't explain at all how I knew this, but I felt it all the same. I turned to Lucifer, no, Gabriel, then.

"Gabriel, please," I said. I swallowed, thinking of how he'd looked at me the night before in the fits of passion. He'd been so tender, and so intense. I didn't think he could truly be so heartless. "Please, if there's a secret society of demon worshippers after me, you can't just leave me somewhere. I'll die! Please."

Gabriel looked at me, and for a moment I thought my plea had got through to him. But then he stood up and shook his head. "My mind's made up. We won't take you back to Jamaica, but the next viable port will be where we let you off. If we can do a ransom exchange all the better. Come on, Dante. You know how I feel about you being close to Cedric."

Dante rose from the bed, gave me a last lingering look. I put on my most pleading, most appealing expression, making my eyes wide and sorrowful. Perhaps he would continue to argue on my behalf?

And then they left me alone again.

But this time my mind was awhirl with what I had learned. A cult. Something called the crawling chaos? It didn't sound good at all. What was going to become of me?

CHAPTER 12

IN WHICH THE ALARM BELLS RING

I must've fallen asleep because I woke with a start, a sharp pain in my hip and a bell clanging loudly in my ears. Some sort of ship alarm, the bell usually rang for change of watch but this was different, more insistent. My hand slipped down to my hip and I found the source of the pain. Something in my trouser pocket.

My fingers dug into my pocket and pulled out a small, hard object. The charm from the sea witch. I peered at it. I'd forgotten all about it... but she'd insisted I take it. She'd said there were people after me, that I should watch my back.

She must have known something. And my dreams certainly haven't been too bad...

I felt I needed to keep it safer than before. I looked around for some piece of string or a bit of leather I could use to secure the charm around my neck.

I got out of bed and started to snoop around the cabin once more. In one of the drawers I found a selection of coiled ropes, soft to the touch and clearly meant for something more sensual than the usual ship's work...

Imagine him using these on me. It'd feel so good...

Swallowing down some of the arousal, but not able to get rid of it entirely, I closed the drawer and continued looking. I'd found a promising looking mending supplies drawer when the door to the cabin opened, letting in some surprising sounds of panic and chaos from outside. That was very unusual. I turned to see Lucifer? Gabriel? Gabriel looking at me. Striding towards me.

"Cedric, get on the bed."

My heart leapt, my arousal flared again. Was this it? Had he changed his mind and he was going to fuck me good and hard all over again?

It was that tone he had that made me want to obey, but I would have wanted to anyway, especially if he was about to undo his trousers and give me a good seeing to. I hopped up on the bed and looked at him expectantly. My heart sped up as he went to the very drawer I'd discovered, the one with the ropes in it.

This is it, it's going to happen, he's going to tie my hands and have his way with me. I don't know what all that noise is outside, but I don't care at all. I just want to be fucked...

He turned back to me, with a heavy looking set of metal shackles in his hand. I nearly fainted.

"Oh, well, if you insist, I'll let you chain me and do unspeakable things to me" I said, my voice cracking a little as my anticipation rose. I held my wrists out to him as he stalked towards me.

"This isn't for pleasure," he said, gruffly, although his eyes had gone darker, and I would have sworn there was a telltale bulge in his trousers, except it wasn't always easy to tell with his penchant for always wearing black.

"It's not?" He closed the shackle around one of my wrists and then roughly tugged it backwards, securing the other one to the end of the bed. This forced me to lie back a little and Gabriel leaned over me, locking the thing with a small key he had around his neck.

My cock throbbed.

"No. You stay in here, and stay safe."

"Safe from what, exactly?" I asked, hoarsely.

"We're under attack from an unknown vessel," he said. Straightening back up, he eyed me, and I fancy he was feeling a little of the same arousal I was.

Distracted momentarily from the titillation of the shackle and the captain's proximity my mind came up against a stone wall at his words. It stopped short.

"Someone's attacking the Devil's Whore? Are they insane?"

Gabriel chuckled, something I wasn't sure I'd seen before. Then his face grew quite solemn. "I'd allow it's not something that happens much at all. But every now and then some pirate will try and prove himself against us... it may get messy, and I don't want them nabbing you for the prize money, so."

He reached down and patted my head, as if I were a dog. "Stay. That's a good boy."

My traitorous and disturbed body even found that exciting somehow, but I managed to swallow down any kind of potentially humiliating reply. Because my tongue wanted to thank him, or promise I'd be his good boy if he wanted me to, or something ridiculous like that.

He left the room, locked the cabin door and I was left to wonder what would happen. I couldn't even continue my search for something to string the charm to.

I wondered what would happen to me if the crew was overcome, but even more, I hoped that Gabriel and Dante would be unharmed.

CHAPTER 13

IN WHICH THE DEVIL'S WHORE IS ATTACKED

*G*abriel locked the cabin door, slipped the key onto the chain around his neck that also held the key to the shackles, and tried his best to forget about Cedric. He had a crew to command and a ship to defend, after all.

The crew were well trained, and as soon as the sails were sighted and the ship's intentions clear they'd rolled out the cannons. He'd taken a risk by going to his cabin, instead of watching for the enemy's trajectory, but Dante could handle commanding the crew. Gabriel wasn't at all sure Dante could handle being alone with Cedric.

Cedric with his soft brown curls, those large, honeyed hazel eyes... the softness of his skin and his -

No.

Putting Cedric from his mind once more, he strode to Dante's side, focusing on his Captain Lucifer persona as if it were a coat he had settled over his shoulders.

"Any idea who they are?"

Dante glanced at him, shook his head, and handed him the spyglass. "None, sir. Marco thought it could be the Ocean's Fury but I think the figurehead's wrong for that."

Gabriel viewed the ship through the glass. He'd seen the

Ocean's Fury once or twice, heard tales of the ferocious captain Maria-Clare. But Dante was right, this wasn't that ship.

It looked like it had once been a Spanish naval galleon, but had some new paint a while back and the mainsail had a crudely painted skull and crossbones on it.

He pulled a face. "Not the Fury, but I don't know who it is. It's almost in range, get the men to prepare to fire."

Dante moved to centre deck and started shouting orders. The men were quick to respond, having drilled and practised many times. Gabriel was serious about his reputation as a pirate and he wasn't about to let the Devil's Whore be blown out of the water.

The enemy ship approached rapidly now, sailing into range and angling their ship forty-five degrees, aiming to come up alongside the Whore. Dante ordered the men on the starboard side to fire when the angle was right and the deck bucked as they discharged and rolled back.

The aim was a little off. One cannonball had smashed the railing at the back of the ship but the others didn't seem to have done more than land in the water.

"Again!" Gabriel thundered. "And aim to sink them!"

The men scrambled to reload the cannons, moving with swift precision.

They fired again, and this time there were some solid hits. A hole punched through the side of the ship that would soon take on water, and another just above it.

But the strange ship didn't return fire. In fact they were sailing faster still, angling as if to ram them.

Gabriel ran to the helm and took it from Bilal, who stayed close in case Gabriel wanted to leave it to them again.

The Devil's Whore was a quick ship, and Gabriel watched as the enemy ship approached, waiting until the last possible moment before hauling on the wheel and skimming away from the trajectory of the other ship. The enemy ship couldn't correct as fast, and they sailed past with just a few feet of space between the ships.

Dante shouted and the Devil's Whore cannons fired again. This time there were screams and the cracking of wood as the enemy ship took damage.

However, it appeared that although they hadn't returned fire, the crew of the mystery ship was determined to board. As they sailed close to the Whore, men swung from the yardarms, using ropes to gain access to the Whore.

Gabriel swore. "Bilal, take the wheel."

He waited until they were beside him, and then ran down to the main deck, unsheathing his cutlass as he moved.

The men who had landed on the deck of the Whore were instantly engaged in battle with Gabriel's crew. The crew were well trained, although they sometimes complained that he drilled them like a Naval Admiral, they all could see the benefit of it at a time like this. Attacks on the Whore were rare, indeed.

The speed with which they moved from operating the cannons to hand to hand battle was impressive, and one that had saved Gabriel's hide more than once.

Gabriel joined the fray with his most terrifying battle cry, a noise drawn from the rage deep within him. Fuelled by the sheer audacity of this enemy to attack him out of nowhere, but bolstered still by the knowledge he had an innocent soul to protect.

Well, perhaps innocent isn't exactly the correct word for Cedric. But he needs protecting all the same. The thought of some stranger stealing him away from me...

Gabriel's vision narrowed from the larger picture to the immediate problem. He ran through an enemy sailor, then side-stepped to intercept another who was making for the Captain's Cabin.

"Not so fast," Gabriel said. "Whatever your quarrel is with me, it's not to be found in there."

"Stay back, fiend!" The man cried. His eyes were wide, wild, and his skin seemed stretched too thin over his wide open mouth. It was a strange enough sight that Gabriel hesitated for a split second. The man lunged forward, a small dagger clutched in his raised hand angled for Gabriel's chest.

The blade fell true, tearing Gabriel's shirt and cutting into his skin before falling to the deck. In a flash the man was gone, tackled sideways by the fleet dark-clothed figure of Dante. He howled in pain and surprise.

Gabriel shook his head, feeling almost as if he were clearing it of some spell or enchantment, before launching himself back into the fray.

Dante pinned the man to the deck, opened his mouth wide to release his fangs, then leaned in to bite the man's neck and drink from him. Gabriel tried not to pay attention to the sight, which wasn't easily forgotten and seemed like something which should only happen in the shroud of night, not in the bright Caribbean sunlight.

Another of the enemy approached, trying to dodge around Gabriel to get to the door of his cabin.

"What on Earth are you trying to get to?" Gabriel shouted, slashing the man across the chest with his cutlass and feeling frustration temporarily overwhelmed by the singing in his blood at the thrill of the fight. The man cried out, more of a howl of frustration than of pain, although he was now bleeding.

"Out of the way," he gasped, his voice hoarse and strained. "Give us the boy!"

Gabriel's blood ran cold.

He gripped the man's shirt with his free hand and yanked him in close, lifting him off the deck easily enough - the man weighed almost nothing - and snarled in his face.

"What boy?"

"Cedric Hale-Harrington," the man hissed. "The boy. We

need him back, we marked him. He's ours for the ritual, to praise the mighty and unknowable one. You must give him to us!"

Gabriel's jaw tensed. His worst fear - that Cedric might fall into someone else's hands, and here it was even worse than that. The enemy had apparently attacked with the single objective of stealing his prize. *His* Cedric.

With a growl of annoyance, Gabriel threw the man down to the deck and sliced his throat open.

He glanced around, seeing that the men from the enemy ship were all attempting to gain the cabin door, and seemed to be mindless of their own pain or danger to their lives. His crew were quickly dispatching them easily enough, but the... the relentlessness of the cultists. Their desperation to get to Cedric left a sour taste in Gabriel's mouth. How could they possibly have expected to survive, attacking the ship like this?

Perhaps they didn't care, so long as one of them got their hands on Cedric?

"Kill them!" he roared, over the sounds of battle and death cries. "Kill them all!"

The battle was over within moments. Another cultist, already badly injured, rushed at him, practically impaled himself on his sword, and died, one hand grasping for the door.

Gabriel swallowed a sick feeling down, withdrew his sword, wiped it on the dead man's chest and strode forward to address the crew.

"They were after our hostage!" he shouted, so that his crew could understand the strange fight a little easier.

Dante rose to his feet, wiping his mouth on his sleeve. From what Gabriel could see of the fallen men, he should surely have eaten well enough to get them to the next port without incident. That was good, at least.

He scanned the deck, taking in the state of his men as he made a plan for what should happen next.

"Marco, take Pilcher and some of the others to loot their

ship. See if there's anything of worth, kill any other cultists you find. If..." a horrible thought occurred to him and he faltered before going on. "If they have any prisoners, and if they do bring them over to the Whore untouched. The rest of you, toss the bodies overboard and clean up. You did well, we'll have rum and revels tonight."

The crew cheered, then got to work. Gabriel sheathed his sword and then went through the pockets of the dead man at his feet. He found a piece of knotted string that could be witchwork, and a strange pendant around the man's neck. No coin or anything of value. He cut the string the pendant hung from and closed it in his fist.

He turned to look at the door to his cabin and felt a surge of protectiveness that was as unwelcome as it was powerful.

Dante stopped beside him. "They were after Cedric?" Dante asked, urgently. Gabriel stood and nodded, showing Dante the pendant from the dead man.

"Members of the cult."

"Fuck," Dante murmured under his breath. "We have to protect him."

Gabriel pretended he hadn't heard, and squashed down the large part of him that agreed.

"Oversee the cleanup will you? I'm going to talk to the man himself."

CHAPTER 14

IN WHICH GABRIEL CLAIMS WHAT HE WANTS

The noises had been properly terrifying. There I was chained to the bed and awaiting possible death, with no way to defend myself or hide if some enemy made his way into the room. I could possibly slip under the bed but the chain would still be there, leading anyone who came in to me.

And besides, I didn't much fancy hiding under the bed as if I was afraid.

I was afraid, of course, but chained up like that there was nothing I could do about it. The ship rocked with the sounds of cannon fire, and then again much worse.

I could hear lots of shouts and thumps, the sound of bodies falling to the deck. We'd been boarded.

I wondered who by? If it was the British Navy I'd be rescued, and I wasn't at all sure I wanted that. Not when I had learned so little about the cursed mark on my back.

The small leadlight windows were tinted with yellow and orange and I couldn't make out which dark shape was a pirate that I knew and which was an enemy.

I heard Gabriel shouting orders, the cries of men in horrible pain and the thumps of bodies hitting the deck.

Something stirred, under my rib cage. A tugging sensation of fear different to my dread of being rescued by boring Naval officers, or the horror that my kidnappers were about to be slain and I was stuck inside.

That was worse somehow. I stuck the fingernails of my free hand in my mouth and chewed on them just for something to do.

I don't want Gabriel to be hurt. Or Dante, come to that. I want them to protect me from whatever's out there. And then fuck me. I want that very much.

The battle actually didn't go as long as I'd thought it might. I heard Gabriel roaring 'Kill them all!' which was properly rousing and I shifted on the bed, wondering if it was deeply wrong that hearing him shout that phrase was somehow attractive. Probably.

Finally, the noises died off and it was just people speaking. Not loud enough for me to hear the details or what the outcome was, except that I was relatively sure I was hearing Gabriel and Dante. Uselessly, I tugged on the shackle, wishing I could press my ear to the door and hear the substance of their conversation but there was no give in it.

It'd be exciting if I wasn't so damned nervous.

Finally there were footsteps and the sound of the key in the door. My heart soared, hopeful. Gabriel stalked in, his expression stony, eyebrows drawn done and mouth set in a tense frown.

His shirt was torn, slashed rather, and there was blood visible on his chest.

"You're hurt," I said.

He glanced down at himself and shook his head. "That's not important." He strode to the bed and stopped next to me, towering over me. I felt my heart speed up and my lips part.

"They were after you," he said.

I shook my head slightly. "I don't understand."

"The cult, that ship, they'd been trying to find you, they tried

to get in here to you. They barely fought, they just wanted...
wanted to get to you." His tone was inscrutable.

I swallowed, mind racing. He had defended me, kept them
from me, killed them all, I had to assume. I had to know why
he'd done it. "Perhaps you should have let them take me, then
I'd have been out of your hair," I said, slowly.

"Don't be an arse," he said. Then he was on me, his mouth
crashing against mine. I surged up to meet him, my free hand
gripping the fabric of his shirt sleeves and pulling him down
over me, so I could touch him with my other hand, laying back
on the bed and moaning with need.

He kissed me until I was breathless and my mind was empty
of anything but him. I wanted more, I wanted him touching me
all over, I wanted him inside me.

His mouth moved to my jaw and his teeth scraped my skin,
his hands were on my trousers, pulling them open and down.

"Do you want this?" He growled from somewhere under my
chin.

"Fuck yes," I said, trying to pull him closer to me somehow
although his chest was already tight against mine.

"Good," he grunted, and his hand closed around my cock.

"You want me?" I managed to ask, although his hands and
mouth were already answering that question. I'm vain and self-
absorbed enough that I wanted to hear him say it.

'Yes, now shut up," he replied. That seemed fair enough,
especially since he'd started to stroke my cock and it felt so good
I just wanted to stop doing anything but feeling it. I decided not
to argue, and just thought about how much I enjoyed his body
on mine.

He ceased the mouthing over my jaw and sat up, pulling my
trousers off and tossing them aside before stripping off his own
shirt. He was sweaty, filthy from the cannon smoke and smeared
with blood. The cut on his chest probably needed attention...

He shucked his trousers off and I sighed gratefully at the sight of his heavy cock and balls. He wasted no time in slicking his fingers with oil and stretching me open. I swore, tugging against the shackle and reaching for his chest - feeling cool where his body had recently been covering mine, my cock aching for more friction but his hands were busy now. One of them pressing my hips down to keep me still and the other pressing into me, fucking roughly in and out to get me open for him as quickly as possible. I whined, scratching at the muscles of his stomach.

"Patience," he said, his voice low and commanding.

"Not something I'm good at," I said, smiling as my fingers found his nipple and tugged on it.

He let go of my hip long enough to bat my hand away, so I closed it over my own cock instead, knowing that he'd punish me somehow, and my eager soul wanting that like an ache.

"No," he gripped my wrist and pulled my hand away. "Do I need to shackle both of your hands, boy?"

I groaned, needy and wanting. "Fuck yes."

He shoved his finger deep into me, up to the last knuckle and I whined again, squirming on him like a fish on a hook.

"No time," he said, dismissively. He kept his hand on my wrist, pressing it to the bed beside my shoulder as he added another finger, wasting no time in scissoring them, forcing me open with the slippery insistence of his fingers. My balls tightened with the pain and the sweet sting of it. "Ready?"

Barely, I thought, and then. *This is going to hurt in the best way.*

"Yes," I said. "Stop stalling."

He grunted out a laugh and withdrew his fingers and pressed his cock into me instead. That gorgeous velvety head filling me and forcing me to give him access where I wasn't properly prepared.

I'd had sex this way before, and although I knew I would feel the sting of it for at least the next day or so, I absolutely coveted it.

He grunted, obviously feeling the tightness as well, and moved his hips infinitesimally slowly, gaining access as I moaned and whined.

"More, yes, please Captain, more," I gasped.

"Captain," he repeated, through his heavy breaths. "Yes, I like that, call me Captain." He pushed in slightly quicker and I felt my body accommodate him, filled utterly with his length. I groaned.

"Captain, fuck, that feels so good."

He smirked, his eyes half closing, leaned in and bit my lower lip, fingers squeezing my wrist in a multi-pronged attack on my senses. I moaned louder, whining with my desire for more of him.

Without warning, he started to move his hips fast, drawing out of me to the head of his cock and then slamming back in. The glorious slide and pull of the withdrawal, the sudden shove back inside, it all had me gasping and quickly on the edge of orgasming.

"Please... Captain... I'm going to..." I gasped.

He let go of my wrist to wrap his hand around my cock, pumping it in the same rhythm he was fucking me. My body had become an instrument he was playing, and it felt incredible.

I wasn't going to last, and he seemed to be encouraging it, so I gave in to the sensations, arched my back on the bed and came with a loud howl of joy. He shoved deep inside as I did, no doubt enjoying the way I was squeezing him. He grunted and I felt him fill me with his hot wet ejaculate.

I fell back onto the bed, panting and stupidly happy with the experience. He thrust a few more times and then pulled out of me, making me whine as he pulled properly free of me. I missed it instantly, although the dripping sensation was sort of enjoyable as well.

Because I'm very easily pleased, I suppose.

The captain leaned over me, plucked the key from around his neck and used it to undo the shackle from my wrist. Then he let the key drop back to his chest and collapsed beside me, his chest heaving as he caught his breath.

"Feel free to do that absolutely any time you like," I said.

Gabriel cut his eyes to me, huffed out his breath and covered his eyes with one hand. "Fuck."

CHAPTER 15

IN WHICH AN ACCORD IS MADE

"Cedric, you absolute nightmare, no," Gabriel said, shaking his head. "I shouldn't have done that."

I rolled onto my side, propped my head up on one hand and used the other to trace the shapes of the muscles on his chest.

Pectoral, deltoid, up to the scalene on the shoulder.

"I'd really like to paint you," I said, surprising the both of us. I'd meant to tell him he was being ridiculous and that of course he should have. But I supposed I'd got caught up thinking of anatomy class, and how the planes of light played so nicely over his body. How I could render him as a hero, standing on the foredeck of the ship, the wind in his hair.

"Paint me?" He sounded amused. I looked up into his eyes and saw laughter, so I bit down the reply about the peach in his skin contrasting with the white gold of his hair.

"Fuck me," I said instead. He practically rolled his eyes, so I continued in this vein. "I like being fucked, you like fucking me, it's the perfect arrangement."

I slowly circled his nipple with my forefinger, smiling as it hardened, betraying his arousal.

"You're my hostage, and I'm going to be paid for you, and Poseidon willing I'll never see you again."

"Tease." I leaned in and licked his nipple, just once, and grinned, seeing his chest stutter when his breath caught. "But if you don't want to, then perhaps I'll see about Dante?" I suggested, keeping my tone light. "He is lovely. Have you ever...?"

"With Dante?" Gabriel's hand found its way onto my back and stroked slowly up and down, petting me like a dog in a way that felt utterly divine. "No."

"Why ever not?" I leaned down and licked his other nipple, then blew on it, so the damp would make the air colder. Gabriel's hand moved to the back of my neck and gently but firmly pulled me back.

"Because it would get in the way of our business partnership," he said. "Nosy little pup. I cannot fuck my quartermaster any more than I can have my way with my prisoners."

"Ah, but you have your way with me," I said. I felt like I'd got him there, and I looked up to see his eyes sparkling with amusement.

"It feels a lot more like you had your way with me," he said. "But fine, yes, I broke that rule with you. That's one of the reasons I need to get you off this ship, which means finding someone to pay your ransom at our next port."

I pulled a face. "Your pillow talk is distinctly lacking in charm, you know."

"It's not supposed to be charming," Gabriel said. He let his hand drop from me and sat up, creating space between us, which was utterly unfair and not at all what I wanted. "It's just the truth. You're a liability, now more than ever. All those men wanted was you, they didn't care about their lives or limbs, they were..." he trailed off, his eyes looking off into the distance and his face contorting into a grimace. "Relentless. For all we know there's more ships out there, more cultists just trying to find you. That makes me and my crew targets, and I can't have that."

I rolled over, facing away from him, wrapping my arms around myself and feeling cold and empty. "Fine."

Gabriel moved on the bed, and for a moment I imagined he was going to wrap his arms around me and tell me it'd be all right. And for a moment I wanted that. I wanted the reassurance and the warmth of him. I wanted his big strong arms around me, keeping me safe.

But after a pause, he got off the bed and I heard him moving about, getting dressed again.

I closed my eyes and told myself I didn't want or need anyone to tell me things would be fine. I could handle whatever was coming, and I certainly wasn't getting attached to a pirate captain who wanted nothing to do with me.

Obviously I didn't need anyone at all.

Except perhaps Oliver. Sweet, innocent Oliver.

Gabriel stopped beside the bed, on my side. I opened one eye and he was fully dressed, back in his black shirt and black trousers. He drew the blanket over me, his eyes crinkled, his mouth softer somehow. He inhaled, as if about to speak and then seemed to think better of it.

I pulled the blanket closer, closed my eyes and pretended to be asleep.

After a few seconds, I heard his footsteps retreat.

CHAPTER 16

IN WHICH DANTE AND CEDRIC CONVERSE

I was out on the deck of the ship, in the cool night air. The stars above seemed to twinkle brighter than usual. I had spent a fair amount of time studying the stars a few years back, when I'd taken it into my head to try and paint the night sky as accurately as I could.

I could hear the waves of the ocean lapping at the sides of the ship. The noise of the blood red sails snapping and fluttering in the wind as the ship sped over the waves.

The smell of the salt spray filled my nose and I breathed out joyfully, feeling at ease with the world and the universe. It was warm and I wore only my underthings, my trousers and shirt probably still on the floor in the Captain's Cabin. It didn't matter, I didn't need those things now.

I looked around for the moon but couldn't see it - perhaps it had already set or perhaps it was a new moon... but as I looked up at the stars, I started to feel ... not afraid exactly but unsettled.

The stars seemed closer than before, closer than I'd ever seen them. My stomach knotted uncomfortably.

That wasn't right.

As I watched the stars, which seemed only a stone's throw

away rather than the millions of light years, or whatever it was that they were, as I watched they seemed to move. The twinkling grew brighter and they seemed to dance from left to right.

Were they moving closer still as they danced?

I took a step back and felt the deck beneath my feet give way, the solid, dependable wooden deck apparently malleable and unforgiving.

I fell onto my back and was trapped, gazing up at a sky that arced impossibly large overhead. The ship around me seemed like nothing, a tiny raft barely big enough to support me. The horizon was close, and the sky was consuming everything, all the space that usually existed, all the air I could usually breathe seemed restricted.

My heart pounded in my ears - it was the only thing I could hear now, and I felt my throat constricting. My skin was cold now, chilled with the oncoming coolness of the stars. The large, tripping stars. I couldn't look away from them, although the light wasn't gentle now, it was piercing, dazzling me.

Filled with dread that became almost overwhelming, I opened my mouth and screamed.

I woke up tangled in the bedsheets, facing the ceiling of Gabriel's cabin, sweat soaking me and the sheets. I thrashed about, panicked, struggling to breathe until I was free of the cursed sheet. I threw it to the ground and wrapped my arms around myself, trying to remember that I was in the real world now and not some horrifying place where the stars were coming for me.

The door slammed open and Dante ran in, his eyes wide and concerned.

"Cedric? What happened?" He raced to the bed and sat down beside me, looking me over.

"I... nothing," I said, a little uncertain as to why he was here, and looking so afraid. "I had a bad dream?"

Dante placed his hand gently on my shoulder and I was struck by how cool the skin of his hand was. It was a welcome sensation, I still felt hot, almost feverish.

"A nightmare? What happened in it?"

I tried to explain it as best I could, but in the light of day the idea of the stars moving towards me didn't seem as threatening as it had felt in the dream. It sounded almost silly. Dante didn't laugh though.

"Was that..." he paused, his eyebrows drawing together. He swallowed, his eyes had dropped to my neck and the bare shoulder he was touching. He lifted his eyes to mine again. "Is that a dream you've had before?"

"No," I said. "No, I've never... my nightmares are usually, I don't know, being married to some dull girl, or Father telling me he's disappointed in me, the usual. Nothing like this at all."

"Hmm." Dante's thumb rubbed little circles into my skin, soothing me. "Perhaps it's linked to your tattoo."

I hadn't thought of that.

Perhaps it was the residual fear of the dream, or perhaps it was the enormity of what he was suggesting - the cult trying to get at me, even while I was on a pirate ship. The tattoo and the permanence of the thing - how could one get rid of something etched into one's back?

Whatever the cause, I was overwhelmed with fright. I threw myself into Dante's arms and wrapped my own around the soft fabric of his shirt.

"Cedric! I can't... the captain..." Dante's body had stiffened under me. His hand dropped from my shoulder.

"I'm rather afraid," I murmured into his front. It was an understatement, but he already seemed rather overwhelmed, and I didn't want to make it worse.

His arms settled around me almost gingerly.

Something about me frightens him, I thought. That idea was so awful I buried myself tighter against him, inhaling his peculiar dry pages scent. A funny thing for a pirate to smell of.

"I'm sorry," I said, not letting go. "I know I ought to be braver, but I'm not. I'm not brave."

Dante's arms tightened around me, and I felt a touch to my hair, his mouth perhaps or his nose nuzzling into my curls.

"You don't have to be anything, Cedric," he murmured. His low voice rumbling in his chest where my ear was pressed. It went some way to console me. "You're in an extraordinary situation and you're coping with it as best you can."

I took a deep breath and sat up a little, keeping close to Dante but pulling back enough to look him in the eyes. In the back of my mind I was realising that I was naked and Dante had his arms around me, but I didn't want to break the spell of his kindness. These tender words he was saying seemed to be hard won, and I wanted as many of them as I could get, especially after how Gabriel had treated me.

"Do you really think so?" I asked, pathetically.

"Yes, I do." Then he leaned in slowly and kissed me on the mouth.

If Gabriel's kisses were fire, demanding, consuming, then Dante's kiss was something more beguiling. A mist perhaps, beckoning one inside, cooling and muffling, while concealing ...who knew what? Both fire and mist had danger associated with them, and I welcomed both.

He kissed slowly, tipping his head to the side and moving his lips as if beckoning something out of me. I opened my mouth to him with a soft sigh.

Unfortunately, that sigh broke whatever spell had been cast between us and he pulled back.

His eyes had become darker, somehow. A deep, seaweed green that promised hidden depths. A tide pool far deeper than expected.

"I can't," he said, although it was barely louder than a whisper.

My fear made me bold, and I climbed further into his lap. "You bloody well can." I kissed him hard, demanding what he had promised me a moment before. Demanding he not only pay attention to me, but give me what I wanted.

Dante kissed me back, his body surged under mine and I felt his hardness, unmistakably large and pressing against my behind.

"God yes," I moaned into his mouth.

This time he didn't just pull back, he pulled me off him bodily, his eyes narrowed, and his lips parted, panting gently. "No, I can't."

I scrambled, trying to touch him again but he shied back from me.

"You don't have to control yourself, I'm asking for it," I said. "I think you're impossibly attractive and you're kind as well, I just want-"

Dante stood up and took a few steps back, putting himself out of my reach. "It's too dangerous, besides, you're the Captain's..."

"I am?" I smiled, pleased despite myself. "I don't mind being yours, too. Unless you'd rather be mine? I'm flexible, I don't mind."

"You don't understand," he said, and he was going to tell me more reasons why the answer was no, but I missed his arms around me and god damn it but I needed that back. My fear and desire were all jumbled up together and now I was annoyed. It welled up in me uncontrollably.

"I do understand, you're afraid of the captain, possibly even afraid of this thing on my back!" I shouted.

His hissed, his face contorting into something pointy and strange, his nose wrinkling. "Don't be ridiculous."

Then he turned on his heel and left the room. I cast around

for my clothes, found my trousers and pulled them on. A hard lump in the pocket. The charm from the witch. She'd said it would guard my dreams.

It hadn't been on my person last night and I'd had that nightmare. I pulled on my shirt and stuffed the charm back in my pocket. I'd ask Gabriel for something to make it into a pendant later, but I didn't think Dante had locked the door behind him, and our conversation was not over. I wouldn't let it be.

I let myself out of the captain's cabin as quietly as I could manage and found myself out on the deck. Quickly I darted along the wall, found the closest door to the deck below and slipped through it.

No one shouted, so I assumed I hadn't been seen. Now I just had to track Dante down.

CHAPTER 17

IN WHICH CEDRIC PURSUES DANTE

I couldn't have told you exactly why it felt so imperative to follow Dante at just that exact moment, except that the opportunity of the unlocked door was too good to pass up. I could have sought out Gabriel of course, but he'd have just sent me back to the cabin.

I could have sought out Marco perhaps? But I still had the taste of Dante on my lips, the alluring coolness of his skin, the way he'd wanted me but pulled away. Perhaps I was wrong and all of this was a mistake? But I'd felt his hardness. The way he'd coaxed my tongue into his mouth and his hands on me, pulling me in. His eyes on my bare skin.

I found the cell where I'd been held previously, the one blanket still in a heap on the narrow cot.

I had to be careful, if the wrong member of crew found me wandering around I could be in trouble.

Thankfully, I heard something then. A growl, or perhaps more correctly a howl of annoyance. And I knew that voice.

I followed the sound to a cabin with the door ajar. I pushed it open, holding my breath, as I took in the sight of Dante tossing a bottle across the room. It shattered into pieces, allowing the contents, which looked like sherry perhaps, or a particularly dark red wine to splash over the deck and the wall.

"Bit of a waste," I said, stepping inside and closing the door behind me.

Dante whirled to look at me, his eyes narrowed and his teeth bared. "Stay back!"

Something in his expression was raw, almost animal and my heart skipped a beat. I pressed myself back against the door, trying to make sense of what about his face was wrong. It was his teeth, I realised. He had too many of them, or perhaps they were too large?

He didn't usually look like that, so I was mostly curious rather than afraid.

"What's wrong with your mouth?" I blurted, before thinking perhaps this was all a stupid mistake and I should have stayed in Gabriel's bed like a good little hostage. There was a smell to this room, and it wasn't of spilled wine. It was something else, something that was familiar but I couldn't quite place.

Dante shut his mouth, brought a hand up to cover his mouth and glared at me. "Nothing. Leave me alone."

"I will if you really want me to," I said. "But after kissing you just now, I rather thought you wanted more, and I definitely want more, so can we just... try that instead?"

"Foolish boy," Dante said. He turned away from me, his shoulders hunched, his back a line of tension I'd have to sketch with the aid of a ruler. All angles and sharpness. "This is for your own good."

"I'm not foolish," I said, then added, "well, most of the time. I'm young but I know what I want. I want you, and I know you want me too, so what's the problem?"

Something clicked into place and I realised then, what the smell was. Blood.

I narrowed my eyes, looking Dante over. He was still turned away, his shoulders moving as if he were breathing hard. He didn't appear to be injured at all though. I looked at the smashed bottle and the rapidly congealing contents. It wasn't wine at all, but something turning viscous and brown.

"Blood?" I breathed. I stepped away from the door intent on investigating. "Was that a bottle of blood?"

"Yes," Dante said. His voice low again. Controlled but only just. There was a tremble in it, something being held back.

"Why on earth would you have a bottle of blood..." I said out loud, and then my own blood ran chill in my veins. "Oh my Lord, you're one of the cultists! You're waiting for the right moment and then you're going to kill me!"

Dante tensed, turned back to me, his expression now one of incredulity, his hand dropped from his mouth which looked perfectly normal now. "Really? That's the conclusion you came to?"

"I'll admit," I said, frowning. "It doesn't make a lot of sense, but... you knew what the symbol on my back meant, you knew I was having a strange dream." I warmed to the subject and spoke a little more confidently. "I don't know why you haven't just killed me, but perhaps you're making sure I'm being delivered into their clutches!"

"I am not a member of a suicidal cult to the old gods," Dante said. He looked at the blood and then at me, sighed and spread his hands out in a gesture of surrender. "I'm a vampire."

I opened my mouth to respond but my mouth was dry and every thought had vanished out of my head.

I closed my mouth again.

"Well?" He raised his eyebrows. "Don't you have anything witty to say about that?"

I swallowed. The magnetism I felt between us, the way he kept staring at my throat. His pallor and the coolness to his skin. I had heard of vampires, in legends and in rumour, but I had no real understanding that they existed.

"Vampire?" I repeated finally.

"Indeed."

I let the implications sink in - he drank blood. He might want to drink *my* blood.

But... I didn't think he wanted to hurt me. I wouldn't have chased after him if I'd thought that.

Although I'd briefly thought he might be from the murder cult, it was a temporary madness. If I thought about it, I knew deep in my soul that Dante wouldn't hurt me.

I trusted him, the way I trusted Gabriel. They were pirates, they were murderers, they were intending to give me back to my family only for a large sum of money, but they had treated me kindly, fed me, made sure no one was taking advantage or abusing me. I felt safe on this ship, if somewhat confined.

Dante might be a blood sucking vampire, but he was loyal to Gabriel and I knew Gabriel to be a good man. An honourable one.

No, these men wouldn't hurt me.

"I don't mind," I said, finally.

Dante's eyes widened. "I beg your pardon?"

"I don't mind," I said again. I took a couple of steps towards him so he could look in my eyes and see how much I meant it. "Okay, so you're a vampire. I like bites, I ask my lovers to bite me all the time. It doesn't bother me. I assume you're not going to kill me, or you'd have said that was the problem."

"It's somewhat implied in the whole being a vampire thing," Dante said. His hand covered his eyes and he sighed, then raised his hand a little to massage his own forehead. "You really have no sense of self-preservation, do you?"

I shrugged and smiled. "Hardly any, or I wouldn't be on this ship with a cursed tattoo on my back."

"Offering yourself to a bloodthirsty creature of the night," Dante said.

"Are you always this dramatic?" I asked, moving a little closer still and smiling, because he wasn't pushing me away now.

"I'm not being dramatic, I'm being realistic. Gabriel has told me no."

"Do you always do what Gabriel tells you to do?" I reached up to touch the smoothness of his cheek. His cool skin made sense now. He didn't move away from my touch.

"Obviously I do, he's the captain."

"If you let him tell you who to fuck then he's more than that," I teased. Dante held my gaze and I could see the hunger in his eyes. His desire swirled there, close to the surface. He pressed his cheek ever so slightly against my hand.

I felt his jaw tense against my palm. "What are you insinuating?"

"Nothing at all. Just that if you let him decide who to bed, you might as well go to him on your knees and ask him to do what he will with you." I probably wouldn't have noticed much of a reaction if I hadn't been so close to him, with my hand on his cheek. But I felt the slight shudder and saw the way his pupils expanded - a sign of pleasure.

"Be quiet," Dante said, his voice low and hoarse.

"Make me," I said, just as quietly.

It was a gamble, but like so many of the things I chose to gamble on, it came out in my favour.

Dante crashed his lips to mine, wrapped an arm around my waist and forced me back against the wall where I moaned, putting my arms around his neck and pulling him in, prolonging the kiss.

His hand slipped down, cupped my rear and squeezed, and my cock responded enthusiastically. I rutted against his thigh - he was a good few inches taller than me, after all, and he was stooping to kiss me.

"God yes." Dante tensed in my arms and I bit my lip. "Sorry, I shouldn't say that, does it hurt you? I don't have a cross or anything."

Dante huffed and covered my mouth with his hand. "Just

shut up. And don't take the Lord's name in vain because yes, it stings." I winked at him so he'd know I understood and then he took his hand away and was kissing me again.

I pushed back against him, trying to aim him for the bed, but his strength, his vampire strength, I supposed, prevented me from budging him even a little. Relenting, I unlaced his shirt with one hand and caressed his chest. He had a chain around his neck with a pendant hanging off it. Some kind of witch's charm perhaps?

Dante kissed my jaw and then very gently nipped it. "Want something, sunshine?" *Sunshine? I don't hate that...*

"Just you," I said, softly. "Possibly on the bed, but I'm open to suggestions."

"Here's fine." Dante lifted me, pressing my back against the wall and yanked my trousers down. "Tell me why you want me."

I slipped my hand down to open his trousers and free his cock, wrapping my hand around him and stroking him. His cock was long, not as thick as the captain's but not narrow. It was a beautiful heaviness in my palm.

"I want you because you're handsome and mysterious and..." I breathed out and tugged on his cock a little more. "Because you're..." I had been about to say something like 'you came running when I had a nightmare' but that didn't seem as sensual and exciting as I wanted to sound. Instead I went with something definitely exciting. "You're dangerous."

Dante kissed my neck. "You're right, I don't want to hurt you," he murmured against my skin.

"I mean, you could bite me," I said. His fingers slipped down my rear and pushed inside without hesitation. I was still aching a little, in the sweet, used way from Gabriel's attention the night before.

"Are you sure?" Dante pushed his finger inside me and I whined with need.

"Yeah, I'm sure, I like bites."

Dante withdrew his finger, carried me to the bed and laid me down. Looking up at him with his dark eyes and his sharp cheekbones and his long dark hair hanging down as if he'd misplaced his hairbrush. My heart skipped a beat but I ignored it in favour of the pulse I knew must be beating in my throat. I tipped my chin up, inviting him in.

"Not yet," he twisted his finger inside me, stretching me open impatiently. His other hand retrieved a pot of oil, and he used it to slick his own cock before bringing it to tease at my hole. "It's best when we're just about to come."

"Ohh." I let my arms drop down to his hips, pressing my fingers into his hips and pulling him closer, pushing my knees up, planting my feet on the bed to give him a better angle for entrance. "Come on then."

He smirked and dropped a careless kiss on my knee before pushing inside with agonising slowness.

"Don't tell me you're going to lecture me about patience," I groaned, although in truth I wanted to be teased. He seemed to know this because he actually moved slower still. His hands moved over my body, feeling me, caressing my skin and focusing on my chest. I gasped as his nail lightly grazed my nipple and he smirked. "Finding my weak spots are you?"

"Has anyone ever told you that you talk too much, Cedric?" he said, his voice a low drawl. His accent had become more pronounced now that he was pressed inside of me. I swallowed hard.

"Yes, obviously, all the time."

He chuckled again. "And you never listen?"

"If I didn't talk as much as I did, I'd never get the things I want," I said.

He frowned a little, considering, and then nodded. He leaned in, pushing my knees apart as he claimed my mouth with his. I reached up to tangle a hand in his hair and pull gently, encouraging him to do more, give me more. He obliged but slowly, seemingly determined to test my patience, what little there was of it.

"Cedric, slow down," he murmured against my lips.

"Why?"

"Because there's pleasure in anticipation." He pulled back from the kiss and pulled himself almost all the way out, luxuriating in the pull and tug of withdrawing before pushing back inside a little quicker. It was a divine sort of feeling - although obviously not Heavenly, after what he'd asked me before.

"You called me sunshine, before," I said, putting on a pout.

He ruffled my hair with his hand and then cupped it at the base of my skull, holding me in place as he buried himself deep inside. He repeated the withdrawal and pushing in several times until I was trembling, biting my tongue so I didn't beg him. I felt sure if I begged he'd simply go slower still and that was the last thing I wanted.

He continued far past what seemed like a reasonable time. "Please, Dante, I need more. Touch me."

He hummed and pressed his finger into my mouth which wasn't at all what I'd meant, but it tasted salty and like the coconut oil and I sucked on it quite happily. He watched me with something like wonder, and I saw his eyes go even darker than before.

My heart sped up, as I imagined what it'd be like when he sank his teeth into me. It would hurt, of that I was sure, but it would also be something new. And something new was always always worth it.

He withdrew his finger and wrapped his hand, slick from my spit, around my cock, starting to pump it very gently. He began to move his hips faster, and I moaned my gratitude. "Yes, please... Go..." I cleared my throat. "Yes, please Dante. More."

"All right, sunshine," he murmured. I felt warmth flood my

chest and my mouth pull into a smile. Damn, for a monster he was being so cute!

I was soon panting and writhing beneath him, wanting more, wanting release, but wanting to feel his bite as well. "I'm getting close."

He shoved his hips against me and started to move at a reasonable clip, fucking me not with the intense violence of the Captain but with enough force to make me grunt when he was fully embedded.

His skin didn't bead in sweat, but his gaze got ever more intense. I felt myself lost in the sensation of his body against mine, and entranced by the strange severity of his gaze. His dark eyes had a sheen of silver to them, I thought. I couldn't look away. Out of the bottom of my eye I saw his mouth open, his fangs elongate under his lip.

Part of me wanted to escape then. A small, prehistoric part of me recognising him as a predator I should try to flee from. My heart accelerated and I shuddered. A much larger part of me wanted to find out what it would be like. If I could surrender to a predator and survive, that seemed like a fantastic adventure.

My mouth was already open to breathe heavily and now I tipped my chin up again, inviting him in.

His hand tightened on my cock and he pumped harder, leaning his head in to breathe against the skin of my throat.

"Do it," I said, trying to somehow present my throat to him even more than I already was.

He shoved his cock deep inside and pierced my throat with his fangs.

It was a bizarre sensation. Pain, for certain, but more than that. A depth to the feeling, which quickly became an ache of pleasure. I could feel him sucking, sucking my blood out of my body and I closed my eyes, gave into it all, and orgasmed hard enough that I thought I'd surely have milked his orgasm out of him.

I wasn't far off. I heard him moan, almost an animal sound, *the apex predator feeding*, and joined him in it. My head spun as he pumped his hips again and filled me with his seed. He shoved deep inside and with something of an effort, pulled back from my throat.

For a moment I felt my blood, hot, spilling onto the skin of my neck. Dante leaned in and licked the wound and the ache dulled to a distant pain. I shivered in his arms, gasping for air and not sure I'd ever be able to get enough again. Dante filling me had felt like everything, especially with the bite. Giving and taking in the same moment, making us utterly linked in a way I didn't truly understand.

I let my eyes flutter closed and gave into the bliss of it all. Dante moved on top of me, licking my neck again, pulling out of me and gently disentangling himself from my limbs. I wasn't about to let him get away though, so I opened my eyes and drew him in with one arm as he settled on the bed beside me. I needn't have worried about him running out though. When I looked into his eyes I saw contentment and warmth and he smiled softly back at me.

CHAPTER 18

IN WHICH THE PILLOW TALK IS SLIGHTLY BETTER

"That was a thing," I murmured.

"You taste... just... delicious, sunshine," he said back, matching my quiet tone.

"Thank you?" I tilted my head to the side and grinned. "Your bite felt... incredible. Transcendent."

Dante smiled wider, showing off those fangs and I felt a thrill of excitement at the sight of them. He seemed much more mellow, more present with me than he ever had seemed before. I liked it, liked him more and more. I stole a kiss from him and lay back, feeling warm through and through.

"Transcendent," he repeated and rested his head on my shoulder. "You are such an enigma, Cedric Hale-Harrington."

"How so?" I raised my eyebrows at him. I'd always prided myself on being very straightforward and direct with what I wanted after all.

"When we planned this scheme, we expected a docile, frightened boy with more money than sense, who would cower in the brig and be minimal trouble. Instead, we got a boy marked by a dark arts obsessed death cult, and aside from all that, a promiscuous mischief-maker."

I flushed with happiness. "Promiscuous mischief-maker, I love that. Put that on my gravemarker, please."

Dante's expression quickly darkened. "You're not going to die."

"Eventually, I assume I will," I said. I let my hand play up his back and stroke his hair, which hung long around his shoulders. It felt soft and smooth, despite the appearance of being tangled or ill-cared for.

"Eventually, but we won't let the cult get to you," Dante said. His eyes blazed a little darker with a possessiveness that went straight to my cock. "I won't let them hurt you, sunshine. I will continue to protect you."

I licked my lips before responding. "I imagine the captain might overrule you on that particular point... I understand he'd still like the prize money for returning me to my family."

Dante glanced at the door, guiltily, and then started to pull away from me, his hair trailing through my fingers. I tried to grab onto it but it was slippery as silk.

"Gabriel claimed you first and now I've..." he swallowed and covered his eyes with his hands. "Fucked everything up."

"Excuse me." I took hold of his wrist and pulled his arm down, which he let me do. I'm confident he had supernatural strength and could easily have resisted if he'd chosen. "You didn't... I'm not Gabriel's property. He well, yes all right, he's claimed me if you want to put it in those words, and it was ridiculously fun, and I want it again but he never said I couldn't go looking for anyone else."

"He has kept you locked in his cabin." Dante tugged against my hold on him, so gently it was like he was encouraging me to grip him tighter, so I did. The point he made was rather a good one and I didn't have an exact counter to the argument. Instead I pulled his hand to my mouth and kissed the tips of his fingers.

"I am in control of my own body," I said, the thought solidifying in my mind as I spoke it out loud. "I get to decide who and when I give access to it." The thought of the confounded tattoo on my back gave my words extra meaning. There was after all, the threat of what the cult would do to my body should they ever get their hands on it again... "And I choose you, and I want to be with you, and yes, I want to be with Gabriel as well. And, if at all possible, the both of you at the same time."

I shivered again, imagining it briefly and then bit Dante's finger gently. Dante's eyes had closed and he intoned a gentle "Ohhhhh..." which was enough like a moan that it encouraged me to continue. Perhaps he had also thought of the Captain in such a light?

"I'd really like to be in between the both of you," I murmured. "Or have you fucking me while he fucked you... that would be..." I groaned, because there weren't exactly words for it.

Dante pulled his hand back and shook his head at me, gently. "We have to talk to him."

"About all three of us, God, yes please."

Dante closed his eyes and his forehead crinkled. "Uh, sorry. I mean, yes, definitely."

"No, we have to tell him what we've done. I'm sure he'll be missing you shortly. It's astounding he hasn't already..."

We both listened for a moment, but there were no shouts from outside the door. My heart sank, and I knew Dante was right. There was no way Gabriel wouldn't miss me, and soon. I felt coldness wash over me as I thought of how cold Gabriel had been with me. I wanted to stay here with Dante, in this delightful bubble of post-coital mellowness. Well, that would require Dante to get back to mellow, I supposed.

He sat up and started pulling his clothes back on, so I got up to do the same, sighing again. Just once on this ship, I'd like a little bit of a lingering cuddle after the fuck.

Once we were both shipshape and Bristol fashion, Dante led

the way out of his cabin. His hand in mine, I assume more to ensure I stuck with him rather than out of any affection.

Although he did call me sunshine and has more or less sworn to protect me. Very curious indeed.

The two of us headed up to the main deck. "Dante, if you're a vampire, how can you go out in the sunlight all the time?"

"A witch did a spell for me, I have a charm for it."

Ah, that explains the thing around his neck.

I squeezed his hand a little and there was a tiny, infinitesimal squeeze back.

Gabriel was at the helm, and Dante strode right for him, which didn't at all seem like a good idea to me, but well, best to get it all over with, I supposed.

Gabriel called some other member of the crew forward. "Kaito, take the helm. I need a word with my quartermaster in private." Kaito had an incredible head of blue-black hair, and shoulders that promised a nice body under his white shirt.

Focus, Cedric. Focus.

"To my cabin with the prisoner, *if* you don't mind." Gabriel said, pointedly directing this at Dante. I could feel the waves of anger rolling off him.

Dante yanked me to the cabin by the arm, we went deep into the room, Gabriel slammed the door behind us and folded his arms, looking at us both.

"Well? I'd like to know the reason our hostage was out on the deck." Gabriel narrowed his eyes at my throat and his apparently fury ratcheted up a few more notches. "And why there are puncture wounds in his neck."

"He came to my room," Dante said.

"Dante came in and then he left and forgot to lock the door," I said, trying to make it sound a little more like it was my fault and not Dante's. "I went looking for him."

"This is why I said none of us should interfere with him!" Gabriel shouted, his voice seemed to reverberate off the walls of the cabin and echo in my ears. "Look at him, we can't give him to his parents with holes in his neck!"

"Those will heal in a day," Dante said. He folded his arms and I shifted my weight, my mouth suddenly dry.

"I feel like I should get to-"

"QUIET!" Gabriel roared. I pressed my lips together and dropped my eyes. "I've said from the start that I wouldn't touch him, and neither would anyone on this ship...Now, this has happened." Gabriel's hand flew up to point at Dante. "I didn't even think you'd be hungry after that bloody cult attack."

Dante dropped his eyes to the deck and shrugged his shoulders. "The boy had a nightmare, it was magical, I could sense it. I came to check if he was all right, it was perfectly innocent."

"You can just call me Cedric," I grumbled. "Not the boy or the prisoner."

"Shut up, *boy*," Gabriel said. "I'm going to deal with you in a moment, I am speaking to my quartermaster."

My ears pricked up at that, thinking of all the variously exciting ways Gabriel might punish me.

Dante swallowed. "He'd had a magical dream, about the cult, and he was terrified, I sensed it so I came to check that nothing untoward had happened, that's all. I didn't think you'd object."

A muscle in Gabriel's jaw jumped as if he were about to burst a blood vessel.

"Perhaps if that was all that had happened I wouldn't have minded. But as it is." He strode over to me and his hand flung out. I thought he was going to hit me so I flinched, but his hand closed on the back of my neck and forced my head back. I opened my eyes to see him peering at my throat.

"Really, it'll be healed soon, Captain. I licked it afterwards, it speeds the process. The mending. Within a day it'll be as if nothing had ever touched him."

I felt Gabriel's hand tighten on my neck. His eyes flicked up to meet mine, and I saw the fury and something behind it. Pain, perhaps? Sadness?

"I'm sorry," I breathed. "I didn't think-"

"Exactly, you didn't think," Gabriel's fingers tightened again and then he let go. I felt my stomach go out from under me. I'd hoped he'd kiss me or tell me it was all right, or possibly jump into bed with me and Dante. "You're going back to the cell."

"To the cell? No!" I shook my head.

"I'm Captain of this ship!" He shouted. I bit my lip. "We're mooring at the next English friendly port we can find and we're getting the ransom for your sorry, over-privileged hide."

He gripped me by the arm and propelled me out of the room. "Gabriel, please," I said, scrambling for the right words. "I don't want to go back to the cell."

"Is it not comfortable enough?" He hissed. "I suppose you got used to my bed, didn't you? Well, no more!"

He led the way down the stairs to the hallway below deck. My heart sank.

"Please, Gabriel..."

He hauled the door to the cell that had previously housed me open and pushed me inside. My skin was hot and prickly at the injustice of it all.

"Now, see here," I said, trying to, well. I was trying to talk him around. I didn't want to stay in this miserable room, and I certainly didn't want him this angry at me.

"I've made my choice," Gabriel said. He had already pulled the door mostly closed, but he lingered in it, looking at me with blazing eyes and a fierce frown. "You are my hostage and nothing more. I shall use whatever means necessary to contact your father and arrange the exchange."

My heart ached, hating the thought of Gabriel selling me back. As if I were nothing more to him than a few coins in a bag. Nothing more than a thing to be sold for profit.

It hurt in my chest, and my stomach. I genuinely enjoyed his company, but there was another matter frightening me.

I was afraid of the cult. I knew he could protect me from their fervour, and on land I had no one.

"Gabriel, please," I said again, my voice breaking a little this time.

I saw something softer cross his face, an expression that might have been something more friendly, something that gave me the smallest flutter of hope, and then he squared his shoulders, huffed his breath out and shook his head.

"My name is Captain Lucifer, and you'd do well to use it."

He locked the door and I was once again alone.

CHAPTER 19

IN WHICH SLEEPING ARRANGEMENTS
CHANGE AGAIN

*T*he stars were close and dancing again. Under my feet the deck shivered lightly. I was chilled to the bone, and I wrapped my arms around myself.

Looking up at the stars, I found my eye drawn to two in particular. They were above me at perhaps a sixty degree angle from the horizon. Two stars that demanded I watch as they swirled around each other, drawing close together, almost enough to touch and then dancing back again. Almost like two magnets attracting and repelling.

I hated it.

From the darkness, the velvet depth behind the star's lights, I thought I saw another sort of movement. Narrowing my eyes I tried to make it out, what could be there beyond the stars? What could possibly?

A being? Another form of star perhaps?

Then I remembered the words Dante had said about monsters and old gods, and my blood frosted my veins, aching suddenly, as if something poison was within me. I shook, struggling to take a breath as my chest tightened and my mouth opened for a scream that wouldn't come.

I wanted to wrap my arms around myself, but with the ache and the pain, my limbs wouldn't respond properly.

The stars dazzled my eyes, waltzing closer in their inexorable pattern, obscuring.... whatever was behind it. Had there been something there? I couldn't see it now.

Something wet slapped itself on the deck near my feet and I knew, deep in my soul, that it was a terrible thing. Something monstrous and weird, something I couldn't understand. Merfolk? No, something stranger than even them.

Tentacles? Perhaps, but no normal octopus, far more likely a kraken or some creature twisted by foul magic....

I wanted, desperately, to look at it, but the stars wouldn't release me. They got closer still, and the slapping squelching noise on the deck did too...

I woke up with a gasp, my body aching. I had no idea how long I'd been asleep but it felt like hours. It was likely dark outside by now.

I wasn't used to the hardness of the cot in the cell, nor the scantness of the blanket. The ship was sailing further North and leaving behind the balmy temperatures of the Caribbean.

Despite the chill, I felt sweat dampening my forehead and soaking my shirt.

"Ugh, fuck," I croaked, sitting up and pulling my shirt off. I used it to wipe my face off.

I patted my trouser pocket but there was nothing there.

That damn witch's charm. I really had to get it back. I didn't at all fancy what would happen in my dream if the stars parted to show what was behind, or the ... thing... on the deck reached my feet. It was all too horrible.

I went to the door of the cell. "Is anyone out there? I need to speak to the Captain!"

For a moment there was no response, and then I heard Marco's voice. "He said no one was to go in or out."

I sighed, rested my forehead on the wood of the door and closed my eyes. Last time I'd had such a nightmare Dante had run to my side. I wondered if the same would happen this time. "Please, Marco. Dante... Dante probably felt that, there's something magic happening. I had a charm, it was in my pocket but I don't have it now."

Marco's voice was closer when he replied, as if he were directly on the other side of the door from me. "I can go ask him, but I have to tell you I don't think it'll go well."

I was too afraid to be angry or brave about it. I felt tears leak out of my eyes at the hopelessness of it all. Here I was tormented by otherworldly monsters and the captain was mad at me for having sex with the quartermaster.

"Please, Marco," I said, letting my voice crack with the horror of it all. "Please, I'm so frightened. Dante will know what it means, maybe, and if he doesn't, perhaps the charm..."

There was a scratching noise, a click and the door opened. I stepped back, bunching my shirt in my hands, before using it to swipe at my eyes.

Marco was looking at me with a sad smile, and eyes that seemed friendly enough.

"I got in trouble last time I let you out," he said. "But I believe that you're really afraid, and I hate that."

I took a deep, rattling breath and nodded, pulling my shirt back on to cover the cursed tattoo. "Thank you, Marco. I'll explain to Gab... to Captain Lucifer... and maybe Dante can help, but there's something terribly wrong and, well." I shook my head. "Thank you."

I moved a little closer to the door, and Marco took a step inside and quite without meaning to, definitely without thinking, I wrapped my arms around him and pressed my cheek to his shoulder. His arms enclosed me with a warm, gentle strength, and the rise and fall of his chest was soothing.

"There, now, you're all right," he said, gently.

He smelled good, like the ocean, and his chest was downy with hair, peeking out from the open vee of his half laced shirt. I closed my eyes and felt his cheek rest on my head.

"Cedric!" Dante's voice echoed down the hallway and Marco tensed, but didn't let go of me. "Are you all right? What happened this time?"

"A nightmare." I squeezed Marco a little closer and then let go of him, and he stepped back, giving me an affectionate smile. I returned it, hoping he could tell how truly grateful I was for the little gesture of kindness he'd shown me.

"Another dream sent from the cult?" Dante asked, his eyes wide and his mouth drawn down in a grimace. I nodded.

"I expect so, similar to the last one. Please, I have a charm, it was meant to protect me from dreams. The witch, she knew, somehow. The witch's charm, it must be in Gabriel's, er, the Captain's cabin and I think the dreams are getting through. It was worse, something new, something I didn't see or understand."

Dante reached for my hand and I took it, but as he led me out of the cell I turned to Marco. "Thank you, truly. You're... very kind." I said, and Marco grinned wide and looked down at the deck.

"It's nothing."

Dante paused to let me talk and then started walking again, his hand tight on mine. "Dante, please, I know the Captain is angry, I just need this charm..."

He glanced at me over his shoulder as he led me up the stairs to the deck. "It's no matter if he's angry or not, you can't be alone when these things happen. It's too dangerous, for you and for the residents of this ship."

I swallowed, because I definitely didn't want to be left alone again, but I felt sure Gabriel would just blame it on my being promiscuous again if I were to suggest it to him. We emerged from the stairwell into the open air and my eyes slipped upwards to gaze on the heavens.

The stars were distant, and didn't seem to be moving, but the sight of them still chilled me all over again. I pressed a little closer to Dante, who made a small noise of sympathy without opening his mouth.

I couldn't be sure what time of night it was. There were few on the deck, but a warm light made the windows in the Captain's cabin glow invitingly.

Gabriel was at his desk, writing in the ship's log. When the two of us entered he looked up with such an expression of weariness I almost turned and left again, only I wanted that damned charm back.

"I'm sure there's a very reasonable explanation for my orders being disobeyed within a day, no, within hours of my giving them," Gabriel said. Then he leaned in and blew on the ink of the log to set it and carefully replaced his pen in its holder.

"He had another nightmare," Dante said, his voice hard. "The forces of darkness move against him. Tell him what the dream was, Cedric."

Dante sort of drew me to the front with a hand on my elbow and I swallowed, looking at Gabriel. He looked immensely skeptical but undeniably dashing in the lantern light. I swallowed.

"Well, Captain, in the dream I'm looking at the stars, only they're not like the stars out there. They're large, they feel close somehow. And they move, like a..." I gestured, swirling my finger through the air, trying to approximate the movement. "And I can't look away from them. This one, that I just had, there was the hint of something behind them."

"Behind the stars?" Gabriel raised one eyebrow and my mouth went dry.

"Yes, sir, beyond them. Something that shouldn't be there, shouldn't exist at all, but. There was movement, and I felt it was coming for me. Then of course, there was the wet thing."

Dante frowned, moving a little towards Gabriel to watch my face. "What wet thing?" He asked, his voice barely above a whisper.

I shook my head. "I don't know, I couldn't look at it. I knew it was coming for me, to do... something awful, I couldn't say what, but my eyes were fixed on the stars. And I was so afraid..." I felt it again, my chest tightening, and my throat constricting.

I knew, with absolute certainty that there was something awful out there that wanted to devour me. The dream, it hadn't been just a dream. It felt more like a terrible promise of something to come.

I covered my face with my hands, because now that I was awake it was as if I could feel the cult trying to get to me, trying to devour me. The tattoo on my back itched and I told myself it was just the sweat, drying on my skin, nothing more.

"I don't think he should sleep alone," Dante said. His voice seemed far away and I realised it was because my ears felt blocked somehow. I dropped my hands and swallowed, trying to clear them.

Gabriel exhaled loudly and crossed the room. He put his hand on my elbow and looked into my face. My breath hitched, and I gulped.

"What good would company do, exactly?" he asked Dante. I felt my eyes tearing up again under his scrutiny. I was so afraid he would turn me down and leave me alone in the cell to be tormented in my sleep.

"He has only had these nightmares when he's been alone," Dante said. "And when he hasn't had some charm off a witch. He said he left it in here, but once we have it back, I'm happy to take him in my cabin, if you prefer that."

"So the two of you can fornicate undisturbed, I suppose?"

Dante groaned in frustration. "Captain, it's not about that, can't you see he's frightened?"

"Yes, I can see that." So gently I hardly believed it was happening, Gabriel's hand stroked up my arm, gently touched my neck and caressed my cheek.

Perhaps he won't send me back to the cell after all, perhaps he will be kind.

"I won't let you bite him again when we're so close to the exchange," Gabriel said. His businesslike tone at odds with his gesture. "He'll sleep in here, and in daylight he can be out on the deck with the crew. None are to touch him, of course. I'll catch some sleep while the sun is high. We're three weeks or so from Casablanca and we have word that there's one there who will give us the ransom."

My heart sank deep into the soles of my feet.

So that was it, he was feeling generous because he knew he'd soon be rid of me.

"He'd still be sleeping alone," Dante said, slowly.

"Who in Casablanca has offered to pay my ransom?" I asked, swallowing down the feeling of loss I absolutely didn't want to feel.

"A naval friend of your father's," Gabriel replied. "We were able to access the witch communication network they use, and arrange to meet them."

"Oh." I supposed that made a certain amount of sense. Father did know a wealth of rich Naval officers, after all, and from Morocco it was more or less north to Dover, although the Spanish waters were dangerous. I felt faint, my previous fears about the cult seeming distant and hardly important at all.

My adventure on the Devil's Whore would be over, and then I'd be stuck on some blasted Naval ship with a friend of my Father's. No doubt asked to dinner with the boring old man each night and all the men on the ship terrified to be seen dallying with me in any kind of interesting way.

"I see," I said.

Gabriel's hand was still on my cheek, and despite the coldness that had washed over me, I pushed against his hand, nuzzling it, and closing my eyes. I wanted him to call me puppy again.

"Captain, the aim is for him to be in company when he sleeps," Dante said. His voice was a lot closer now, and I opened my eyes, wondering if, somehow, this would be the moment when we all fell into bed together and tumbled one another in all sorts of ways. Dante's voice turned even more appealing, smooth as fine velvet and dark as a plum. "Trust me. He needs our protection, or the cult will locate him and the ship. We may not be as lucky the next time they attack."

Gabriel dropped his hand from my face and turned to Dante. He gazed at him with something intense, something powerful. My mouth went dry, anticipating...

"Then he shall have company," he said. "When it is time for him to sleep, I shall be here, or if I'm needed on deck you will be. But I absolutely forbid the biting and feeding."

"I understand, Captain."

"You may go."

I gave Dante a tight smile. "Thank you, Dante."

Dante hesitated, perhaps about to suggest something? But then he closed his mouth into a thin line and left the cabin. I cast around for the witch's charm.

"What are you doing?" Gabriel asked, and I thought I detected a slight hint of amusement in his tone so I decided I could probably be a bit cute with him instead of snapping to attention.

"Before you sent your men ashore to kidnap me, I was in the market and a sea witch sold me something." I said. Then I got on my hands and knees and aimed my ass at him as I searched around on the floor. I hoped I was presenting myself to my best advantage. He didn't respond so I continued to talk, taking on a

109

casual, conversational tone. I crawled towards the bed to feel under it. "She seemed to know an awful lot, she said that there were people following me, and the charm was to protect my dreams or something. It wasn't in my pocket either time I had the weird horrible dream. Ipso facto, I need the charm back."

"Is it this?" Gabriel asked, once I'd sat back up on my heels. I turned to look at him. He held the sea witch's charm aloft.

"Yes, brilliant! Thank you, where did you find it?"

"It was on the floor, so I put it beside the bed," Gabriel said. "You may have it back, if you ask nicely."

I was still on the floor, and I didn't hate the feeling of being on my knees before him, so sat up, put my hands on my thighs and looked up at him, as prettily as I could. "Please, Captain, may I have it?"

There was a familiar shine in his eyes and I saw a bulge in his trousers and my mouth watered in response. He smiled, a wicked, piratical smile that sent a wave of heat through my body.

I crawled closer on my hands and knees and tried to look fuckable.

When I got nearer something changed in his expression and he huffed his breath out. The smile vanished and he tossed the charm to me and turned away. "If you wish to come out onto the deck, you're welcome. I'd best get back to my duties."

I caught the charm and my heart sank into the floor. I bit back the disappointment and pulled myself to my feet. I didn't want to lose the charm again.

"Well, if you won't fuck me again, have you at least a piece of string or something so I can hang this thing around my neck?"

Gabriel had been halfway out of the cabin, but at the word 'fuck' he stopped walking. "There's ribbon and cord in there," he said, pointing at a small wooden box on the shelf. "Help yourself."

Then he squared his shoulders, lifted his chin and left the

cabin. It was at least a refreshing change that he didn't lock the door behind him. I pulled out the box and sorted through.

Captain Lucifer's ribbons, what a thing. The leather thong would last longer, but wouldn't be nearly as stylish. Fuck it, I'm taking a pirate's ribbon.

I felt positively whimsical as I picked out a slim black satin ribbon and tied it securely around the charm and then hung it around my neck. I tied it so it hung in the centre of my chest, sort of over my heart. Well, near it anyway.

I pulled my shirt closed and fastened it over the charm. Then I found Gabriel's comb and dragged it through my curls. I sighed, and wondered if I could ask for a bath. Only one way to find out, I supposed...

CHAPTER 20

IN WHICH THE CREW OF THE DEVIL'S WHORE
ENDURE CEDRIC

*T*he next three weeks were a varied lot. In some ways I found them were very pleasant, as I had my freedom to wander the ship's decks and get to know the crew.

Simply being able to breathe the fresh air and get some sunlight on my skin made a world of difference to my frame of mind.

I got to know Marco better, as a friendly face, his was the first I gravitated towards. I also learned the strange truth about him, that he was a magical being. An otter who could turn into a human.

"I beg your pardon," I'd said when he first told me.

Marco grinned back with a mischievous sparkle in his eyes that appealed to me deeply. "Some might say I'm a shapeshifter, or a man who can become an otter, but that's the wrong way around," he said. "I'm an otter who chooses to be human some of the time."

"And serve on a pirate ship," I added, hardly able to process his words. "How is such a thing possible?"

"Captain Lucifer takes in all sorts of waifs and strays," Kaito said, appearing at Marco's elbow. "I heard you found out about Dante?"

"I, er, yes, I did." I glanced over my shoulder, half expecting Dante to be looming over me. I saw him talking with Gabriel at the helm.

My hand went to my throat, and both Kaito and Marco eyed the gesture and looked at each other significantly.

"I seduced him," I said, quickly. "Not the other way around."

"That makes sense, he's very careful most of the time." Kaito nodded slowly. He was another handsome man, wearing a slimly tailored white shirt with a silk vest over the top. The silk was brocade, an amethyst colour, with a pattern of leaves and cranes over it. My fingers itched to recreate it in a drawing and then a painting. I wondered if I'd ever be able to blend paints to reproduce that shining purple.

"I say," I said, utterly distracted by the fineness of his clothing. "I don't suppose there's any paints or canvas on board this ship?"

Marco tipped his head to the side and made an amused noise and Kaito shook his head.

"No, although I believe the Captain has some watercolours for map making, somewhere. I'm sure you could get parchment and a pencil of some sort. Dante would know, as the Quartermaster, he'd have the records."

I smiled, pleased to have a reason to seek out Dante in particular. Then I remembered Marco's revelation. "No, I simply must know. How does an otter become a human?"

Marco laughed and shrugged. "No idea, honestly, I just learned how to do it one day, maybe six years ago."

"Most likely it was a curse from a witch," Kaito said. "But this simpleton doesn't remember it."

"I remember meeting the Captain though," Marco said, smiling, possibly unaware that Kaito had just insulted him, or maybe he simply didn't care. "I was trying to get some food at some big manor house, and he was there pretending to be a gentleman. Together we stole seven necklaces, two deeds of ownership and a diamond ring."

I blinked, trying to imagine such a thing. "I expect being able to shapeshift to a smaller size makes thieving easier?"

Marco nodded and beamed. "Exactly. And that's how I got my job."

I laughed, Marco's happiness was quite contagious.

My next mission was to talk to Dante, so I made my way up to the helm. Dante and Gabriel ceased talking as I approached, which I hardly minded, I was in such a fine mood.

"Good afternoon, gentlemen. I understand that might have you have watercolours on the ship, possibly?" I said.

Gabriel's eyes narrowed and he frowned. "Damn it." He dug a coin out of his pocket and handed it to Dante, who smiled wickedly as he took it.

"What was that about?" I asked.

"Gabriel thought the only reason you'd approach us would be to ask for sex again," Dante said. "I said you'd have something else you wanted."

"Wait, are you saying I could have asked for sex just now? Because I'll do it. If I do, what's the chance you'd both say yes?"

"Too late now," Gabriel said, a glint in his eye that looked more joking than angered. "I'm annoyed about losing coin to Dante."

I shook my head and sighed. "I see you are both united in teasing me, and not in the fun way without clothes. Well, what to my original question then?"

Gabriel smiled slightly and looked out to the horizon.

"Yes, I believe we have some paints on board, why on Earth do you want paint?"

I speculated that suggesting something salacious such as using a damp brush to apply paint to Gabriel's skin from toe to head wouldn't go down well, so I opted for an honest answer.

"Something to while away the time. I'd love to try and

capture each of the crew in portrait, if you have the paper available for such a project?"

Gabriel snorted and I looked over to see him smiling for real, amused at me. "You never stop surprising me, Cedric."

I took that as a compliment, nodded my thanks and turned back to Dante.

"I'll go and have a look for it," he said. "You wait up here."

And then I was able to spend a good few hours before dinner sketching the captain in all his glory at the helm, and making good use of the small tin of black paint to capture the folds of his clothes.

So my days were spent rather blissfully, sketching handsome men of the crew, painting and making friends with the residents of the Devil's Whore. In stark contrast to all the stories and the things I'd been taught about pirates, they were all rather friendly men and perfectly happy to make conversation with me.

I'd dine with the crew, and was well entertained by their stories and songs, and I went to the cabin once they went back to work.

Gabriel was true to his word and he stayed in the cabin with me as I slept. In fact he slept beside me in the bed, which was deliciously comfortable and warm. And although I snuggled against him, and sometimes I woke with his arm around me, we did nothing more than that. Not a kiss, and definitely not any touching.

I savoured those sleepy moments pressed against his warm body even though I knew I wouldn't get anything more. I felt so dreamily content with his arm around me. I felt as if nothing could ever hurt me, that I was in his protection, which was absolute. I slept very soundly.

. . .

Finally, the day came when Gabriel informed me we'd be landing in Casablanca to make the exchange. That's how he put it. We were standing in his cabin, me pulling my shirt on in order to be dressed for breakfast and him already fully clothed in all his blackest, most piratical gear, ready, I assumed, to go on land and claim payment.

"The exchange?" I said, as if I didn't understand.

"You will be returned to your family, and I will take the payment," he said, lightly. His tone betrayed something in his eyes, I thought. Perhaps he wasn't truly happy to be rid of me?

"I can't believe you'd so willingly part with me," I said, knowing I sounded petulant. "Sleeping beside you has been so pleasant, and several times I've woken with your arm around me. I think you enjoy it too."

"I have no idea what you're talking about," he said, and turned away to fuss with his compass. I sighed, because it was clear he'd made up his mind.

"Well, I hope the cult has given up on me, because there's no way some friend of my father's can fight them off."

Gabriel's shoulder's stiffened at that and he cleared his throat. "No sign of them for days. Perhaps the charm stops them tracing you." And then he stalked right out of the room, like we hadn't been in the middle of a conversation.

I huffed a little at the general indignity of it all, and then followed him out. I wanted to say goodbye to the crew after all.

I started by seeking out Dante, since I was closest to him after Gabriel. He was in his cabin, doing something with the ship's records. His hair was swept over his shoulder on one side, exposing the long, pale line of his neck.

I'd spent a very enjoyable few hours the day before sketching him, studying the planes of him, and getting steadily more aroused, but he'd obeyed the captain and largely ignored me.

I'd tried to pretend I didn't care when he ignored me.

He looked up as I entered the cabin. His face went through a few different expressions and then settled on careful disinterest.

"Good morning, Cedric."

I felt a little nervous, suddenly, my heart thumping in my ears. "I uh, I understand that I'm leaving you all today," I said, feeling ridiculously formal.

Dante dropped his eyes to the ledger and wrote something. "Indeed."

"So I wanted to say goodbye to you, because, well, you know." I moved closer to the desk, practically daring him to look me in the eye and act so dry and disinterested. He set the pen in its holder, folded his hands and looked up at me.

"I'm most likely in the party taking you ashore," he said. His voice was low and measured, controlled. No emotion leaking through. "But I appreciate the gesture."

I hadn't given thought to who would be escorting me to shore but of course, someone would. I wondered how they'd do it...

"Dante, you really don't have to be so formal, you've literally been inside me and drunk my blood."

Dante cleared his throat. "Cedric, I'll miss you, I'm sorry we have to give you back, but the Captain has made his orders very clear. There's nothing to discuss."

"So you *do* like me!" I planted my palms on the desk and leaned in, grinning with triumph. Dante leaned back ever so slightly.

"Yes, I like you, and I'm afraid for your safety with that tattoo marking you. But as I said, orders are orders."

"Fine, at least give me a kiss before I'm banished from the ship forever." I leaned further across the desk.

Dante hesitated, and I knew he was imagining Gabriel's reaction if he found us kissing. Thankfully, he also appeared to be weighing up the benefits of kissing me because he leaned in and did it.

I closed my eyes, hungry for more as soon as his lips touched mine. I bit back a moan and took it for what it was, a peace offering, or a goodbye or something like that. Dante wouldn't disobey the Captain, but I could have this at least.

"Thanks for saying you'll miss me," I said, a little softer than I'd been speaking. I felt suddenly, and strangely on the verge of tears. I swallowed a lump in my throat and forced myself to smile.

Dante's hand was on my jaw, his thumb rubbing my cheek softly and he smiled indulgently at me. "Best of luck for the future, Cedric. I really will miss you." He dropped his hand and cleared his throat, breaking the spell of tenderness. I straightened back up.

I looked him in the eyes and he looked back at me with sad fondness. I wanted so much to say more, but I had no idea what it ought to be. My stomach dropped away and the lump came back to my throat.

It doesn't matter, I told myself. *Just move on.*

"Right, uh, I'll see you soon, I suppose." I turned and left the cabin, feeling my eyes misting. I swiped my sleeve over them as soon as I was out of sight of him. It took me a few moments to get myself under control, and I had to give myself a stern talking to.

Yes, Dante likes me, yes, he'll miss me, and I'll certainly miss him, and think about that bite and the fucking and all of that. But there's nothing for it. Lucifer is going to get his ransom and he can't have that while I'm still on the ship. This was never a long term arrangement, and I knew that.

Saying goodbye to Marco and Kaito should have been easier, but it really wasn't. The two of them had been kind to me, and allowed me to draw them multiple times each. Marco had even shifted into his otter form and let me draw that too, which was rather special. I'd never seen a sea otter before, let alone had a magical one pose for me.

I'd done several studies of Kaito, trying to capture the colours in his clothes and never quite coming close. The pigments in the watercolours weren't bright enough.

They were kind about saying goodbye, but they were a little cold as well. Marco smiled but it didn't reach his eyes.

"Best of luck for the future," Kaito had said, and then turned away.

I felt like a wrung out rag when I retreated back to the Captain's cabin. I'd seen land on the horizon, and it wouldn't be long until we were mooring. Just a couple of hours.

I felt like I was being taken to prison, rather than released from captivity.

I went to the desk where I'd taken a small amount of space for my paintings. I sighed, flipping through the pages of portraits I'd made. I'd have to leave them on the ship. There was too much care in the execution of them. If anyone saw them on land they'd see the affection I had for all these men.

I left them in a neat pile and went to settle on the bed, miserably awaiting my fate.

CHAPTER 21

IN WHICH THE RANSOM IS COLLECTED

*A*s they sailed towards Casablanca, Gabriel looked over the deck and nodded his approval. The Devil's Whore was obviously a pirate ship most of the time. Gabriel liked to declare it vividly, because with the reputation he'd built up for Captain Lucifer, most saw the ship with the red sails and avoided it.

But when the red sails were taken down, and replaced with the white canvas ones, it looked much like any other privateer's ship. Gabriel found it too time consuming to change the sails too often, but Casablanca was close to Spain and Britain, and the waters were more frequently patrolled than those in the Bahamas, so it had seemed worthwhile to do it this time.

Plus, Gabriel thought, it was a handy distraction from the sorrow and drama that Cedric was creating by going around and saying goodbye to the crew.

In the time they'd had him on board the ship, Cedric had made an impression. He was impossibly charismatic. Both impossible and charismatic, yes. And Gabriel knew in his heart of hearts that he'd miss the boy, too. It had been a lesson in patience and agony to hold himself back from Cedric carnally, especially when they were lying in bed together. He'd tried to wait until Cedric was asleep before getting into bed with him, that made it a little easier but as he slept, his body betrayed his true desire. He'd awaken with his arm around Cedric, or pressing his nose against his shoulder, inhaling the sweet scent of the boy.

His ridiculous, adorable puppy.

Pathetic, he told himself. The crew needed the ransom money. He had promised them riches and celebration, and to do those things they needed the money Cedric's father's friend had secured to pay him off.

He made sure he was wearing his most impressive Captain Lucifer garb, brushed his hair back and tied it with a black ribbon and had Marco shine his boots until they reflected his face. Perhaps emerging from the ship looking like this would alert someone to the fact that it was a pirate ship, but it had never happened before. And Sir Gabriel Durant couldn't be seen to be involved in a kidnapping.

A generous addition to the mooring fee usually meant no one asked questions he didn't wish to answer.

With Kaito at the helm, the ship would dock within the half hour. It was time to stop avoiding his own cabin and prepare Cedric for the handover. Perhaps he should just have Marco handle it and avoid Cedric himself.

He considered that option for a moment and quickly dismissed it. If Cedric wasn't allowed to be dramatic and emotional at him now, in private, he'd certainly attempt it later on. Best to get it over and done with so that things on shore would be more or less seemly.

As they got closer to the mooring, he went into his cabin.

Cedric was sprawled dramatically on the bed, one hand thrown over his eyes and the other arm out to the side.

Since he knew Cedric wouldn't see it, Gabriel allowed himself a smile. The boy was beautiful, his dark curls spilling over the pillowslip, his hip bone jutting up in an inviting way, torso canted slightly to one side due to an artistically bent leg.

Gabriel cleared his throat.

Cedric didn't move, apart from his mouth. "I heard you walk in. I expect it's time to get your money for me, is it? I didn't feel the ship moor just yet."

"Soon," Gabriel said. "Are you ready to go?"

Cedric sat up, letting his arm fall away and fixing a baleful gaze on Gabriel. "Funnily enough, I didn't have much to pack. On account of how you kidnapped me off the streets and I have nothing of my own here."

Gabriel found himself looking away from Cedric, feeling slightly guilty. Or possibly quite guilty indeed, so he distracted himself by looking through the sketches and portraits Cedric had made of the residents of the Devil's Whore. They were really quite beautiful.

"This is fine work," he said, honestly. "Do you not wish to take one or two?" He imagined Cedric with his sketches of Dante and Gabriel, dreaming about the two of them, and then tried to dismiss the thought, although it wasn't easy.

He turned back to Cedric, who had raised one eyebrow. "Do you really think I want someone to find flattering portraits I made of my captors, just, kept in my bedroom in the manor house, or secreted about my person? Would raise some questions wouldn't it?"

Gabriel allowed that it would. "Perhaps you're right."

"I hate this, I hate goodbyes," Cedric said, his voice deceptively light. Gabriel suspected there was a quiver of emotion under the words. "I don't want to go, and I don't truly believe you're as indifferent to me as you pretend."

Gabriel sighed a breath out before he considered that it might be giving away more than he meant to.

"Come along, Cedric, you're not suited for this life, and we took you for one reason and one only."

"Yes, to be paid. I know, I know. Well then, what do you want me to do, go sit in the longboat and wait for father's old shipmate to claim me?" He stood up and squared his shoulders, gazing up at Gabriel as if challenging him to do something.

But to do what? Gabriel wondered. *To kiss him? To tell him he was sad to see him go? I cannot do such a thing, then I might weaken, be selfish and decide to keep him. I need that money.*

"For now, you can wait here." Gabriel felt his arm twitch, he wanted to touch Cedric's curls one last time, to caress him, to hold him close. He squashed the desires down and folded his arms. "Marco will come and get you when it's time, Dante will be with him. They'll bring you ashore to the designated meeting place once I've secured the ransom."

"Lovely." Cedric's lip curled and his eyes flashed cold as Gabriel had ever seen them. "I hope you enjoy your payment."

Such a barb shouldn't have had any effect on Gabriel, but his gut twisted in an unpleasantly liquid way at Cedric's words. He turned and left the room, cursing silently at the power the boy had to get under his skin.

Gabriel strode down the gangplank and onto the marina, tipped the harbourmaster well to register the ship under the name *The Blue Mermaid* and made his way to the designated meeting place. The witch's network was a marvellous invention, Gabriel mused as he made his way to the inn the man had named. In previous years, before the British Navy had recruited witches, such a ransom exchange would have involved letters and days of waiting, not knowing if a missive had got through or not. This was much more convenient.

The inn was named simply Azul, and there were a group of men out the front sharing a tall glass pipe contraption that Gabriel had seen before, a way of combining tobacco with water somehow, which seemed to be a marvellous invention, as well.

Inside the inn it was short work to spot the man in the British naval uniform. Gabriel approached him, checking the other denizens of the bar. He had his cutlass on his hip, and various other weapons concealed under his coat, but it always paid to check the surroundings to avoid being surprised.

There were few people in the bar, and most of them looked like residents of the town, or Portuguese sailors. None were paying him any attention aside to look at him and then quickly away again.

That was how he liked it.

The man, Cedric's uncle, didn't look terribly appealing, but then, he was some sort of Naval officer, and Gabriel had never found them appealing. Gabriel stopped at the table and eyed the man.

"Chief petty officer Roderick Wright?" Gabriel asked, his voice low.

"Indeed," the man nodded at the chair and leaned forward on the table. "Cedric, is he alive? Is he well?"

Gabriel sat down, leaving one hand on the hilt of his cutlass. "If you have brought the payment, you'll have him returned complete and healthy. If you have some sort of double cross or deception I can assure you he'll not remain in one piece." He let his voice get a growl to it, the menace that had got him what he wanted so many times before.

The man, who was already pale, nodded, his eyes wide. "Of course. I'd not dare to... I understand your reputation mister...er, *Captain* Lucifer and I have no desire to witness your ire."

Gabriel gave him a cold smile. "Then we're agreed. I'll be needing the money up front of course. Then you can come down to the docks and retrieve the boy."

The man was clearly nervous, perhaps more nervous than Gabriel had expected of a Naval man. He fumbled a little as he picked up a canvas bag from the chair beside him, he put it on the table between them, and it made a satisfying clinking noise.

Gabriel used his left hand to pull it open so he could look inside. The pile of coins inside was a mix of Spanish doubloons, French francs and British pounds. He could hardly count each one here, but he pulled one out at random and tapped it on the table. It rang, true and clear.

He did a little mental arithmetic and decided it looked like enough to meet his ransom demands.

"All right. Here's what we'll do," he said, leaning forward to speak quietly. "Come down to the East docks in thirty minutes. I'll take this aboard, count it and confirm it's enough. If you've short changed me in any way, we sail off." *And I get to keep Cedric,* he thought to himself. He cleared his throat and focused again on the man in front of him. "If it's the amount we agreed on, then I'll send a couple of men out with Cedric and the deal is done."

"Of course, Captain. That will give me time to bring my carriage around. I imagine after his ordeal with you, he'll appreciate not having to walk too long."

It was an odd thing to say, and Gabriel frowned, his eyebrows drawing together. But there was nothing truly untoward going on. The man was wearing a British Naval uniform, he was in the place to meet Gabriel and he had the money. There was no particular reason to doubt his motives. It wasn't as if some slave trader or cultist could have intercepted the message he'd sent through the Naval network.

"Right." He stood up, picked up the canvas bag and tied it to his belt, letting the jacket fall over it. "Thirty minutes."

"Thirty minutes."

He turned and left the inn, making his way back to the ship using a circuitous route to the West docks. With each step the feeling of unease faded. He kept his hand on his cutlass, just in case some pickpocket decided to try his luck, but no one approached him or even looked him in the eyes. The people had their own business to mind.

He was so close to succeeding, he had the money in his possession. It was going to be quite the pay for all the crew, and himself included.

Simple, and relatively victimless crime. There'd been some drama of course, but Cedric would soon forget them. He had a great future to look forward to, returning to his family in London in due time, no doubt he'd eventually meet his match and settle down with a nice girl and this whole adventure would become a story he'd tell his children and then grandchildren. They probably wouldn't even believe him...

He smiled as he saw Kaito, keeping watch from the prow of the Devil's Whore. It would be better for everyone with Cedric gone. Less distractions, and far less drama. Yes, this had been a wonderful plan he'd thought up, planned and just about executed.

He stepped lightly up the gangplank, went to Dante's cabin and set the bag of coins down in front of him.

Dante sighed, because Gabriel had just put the bag down on the ledger, and possibly smudged the writing he'd been doing.

Gabriel smiled at him. "Count it, make sure it's all there."

Dante set his pen in its holder and pulled the bag open and started to count it, setting the coins down in little stacks. It added up quickly and Gabriel felt his cheeks start to ache with the width of his smile.

Dante emptied the bag. "There's actually a little extra, Captain."

"As it should be, if they want their boy back," Gabriel felt almost giddy. "I'll secure that, and you and Marco can take Cedric to his father's friend, I told him to wait with his carriage a the East docks, on the far side."

He scooped the coins back into the bag and tied the neck of it. He waited for Dante to stand and then led the way up to the deck. Marco was lounging in the doorway to his cabin, looking in and chatting with Cedric.

"Marco!" Gabriel called. "It's time, they've paid up and we'll celebrate tonight!"

Crew members from around the ship cheered at his words, and Gabriel smiled even wider, ignoring the look Cedric was attempting to give him. He suspected it was reproachful and would ruin his mood.

"Come on, then," Marco said. He gestured to Cedric, who got up slowly.

"Wonderful." Cedric stood up and stretched his arms over his head. Gabriel didn't look away from that, he watched as Cedric's shirt rode up and exposed a strip of his stomach. The pose, with his hands over his head, reminded Gabriel of fucking him while he pinned him down.

Gabriel felt his cheeks warm with the memory, and with the thoughts of other things he'd be able to do to Cedric, should he stay on the ship.

But that was ridiculous, he'd taken the payment.

Of course, he was a pirate. It's not like anyone would be surprised if he backed out on a deal...

But crossing the British Navy so close to their own waters would be suicide.

Marco moved out of the doorway and Cedric walked through. To Gabriel's annoyance the crew all called out to Cedric.

"See you!"

"Try not to get into more trouble, Ced!"

"By 'Rick!"

"We'll miss you."

Cedric smiled and waved at them like he was a member of the royal family. Gabriel's temper bubbled over.

"All right, that's quite enough!" The crew went quiet and Cedric dropped his hand to his side. "Dante, if you please, remove him from the ship now. Officer Wright should be at the East docks with a carriage of some sort."

Dante took Cedric by the arm. "Come along then," he said.

Gabriel was grateful he hadn't taken him by the hand. He watched as Dante and Marco escorted Cedric down the gangplank.

Cedric glanced over his shoulder at Gabriel. "No goodbye kiss?" it was a question but delivered as a barb, an insult of a kind.

Gabriel remembered when they'd brought him onboard, unconscious and sweet looking, his eyes closed and his curls falling into his face. He'd had no idea of what Cedric awake would be like.

His heart thumped dully. He'd miss him.

He went to the prow of the ship to watch as the handover occurred and tried to regain the excitement and elation he'd felt getting back aboard his ship.

CHAPTER 22

IN WHICH THE HOSTAGE IS RETURNED TO
DRY LAND

*A*ll right, so saying "no goodbye kiss" to Gabriel was
definitely a barb. The kind of sniping you'd expect at
some high society dinner where one of the guests hated one of
the other guests for getting engaged to the wrong person.

But I had to have the last word, one way or another. This
might well be the last time I ever saw Gabriel, or any of them,
and I wanted them to remember me.

Marco chuckled and shook his head. "I'll give you a kiss
goodbye if you like."

"You will not," Dante said. His hand tightened on my arm
and I allowed myself to enjoy that ever so slightly.

"That's very sweet of you, Marco," I said, surprised. "Perhaps
in other circumstances I'd accept that offer, but unfortunately, in
this particular situation, I don't actually feel like taking you up
on it."

"Ah well," Marco said, lightly. "Maybe some other time."

I looked around as we got down to the moorings.
Presumably the friend of my father's was waiting to whisk me
away, back to my old life. What a dreary thought. Every step I
took away from the Devil's Whore made me feel heavier, more
despairing.

At least I could look forward to seeing Oliver again, that thought was the one spark of hope.

We were already nearing the East docks, and I cursed Marco and Dante for walking so fast. There was a carriage on the street, a few hundred metres away. A tall man in a British Naval uniform stood nearby it.

"That's the one," Dante said, and steered me towards the man and his carriage. There was a fair amount of traffic on the street, people unloading things from their ships, people with handcarts full of wares, heading into the city. People wearing clothes from all sorts of different cultures. The Englishman rather stood out.

The carriage he stood by looked a little unusual too, as most people had open pony carts or barrows. The dark stained wood stood out against the buildings.

The man wasn't at all familiar to me, which wasn't entirely surprising. I didn't pay an awful lot of attention to my father's friends and he didn't often host them at our London house. He perked up when he saw us approach, which was promising.

Dante squeezed my arm again. "Cedric," he said softly. I looked up at him, frowning.

"What?"

"Stay safe. These people who are after you..." he trailed off, took a deep breath and sighed, his expression tormented. "Just, try and stay out of trouble."

My heart ached, and all I wanted in that moment was to reassure him that I'd be fine. I didn't believe it at all, but I hated the thought of leaving Dante with a whole lot of drama and sadness so I plastered a smile across my face and winked at him.

"Don't be ridiculous, old man," I said, as cheerily as I could manage. "Not to worry. The Navy will protect me, and then I'll be back in London and hitting the clubs again. And not the weird sex cult ones, I promise."

Dante didn't look entirely comforted, but he slid his hand

down my arm, to my hand and squeezed it tight. Out on the streets of this unknown port I expected he didn't feel comfortable kissing and hugging me.

Well, I didn't care. I threw my arm around his neck and kissed him, hard but brief, because as soon as I was kissing him I didn't want to stop, and I knew I must. My throat closed with unshed tears and I felt them welling behind my eyes.

Ridiculous, utterly ridiculous.

I let go of Dante and turned to Marco. "Make sure the Captain doesn't do anything stupid like get himself killed. This one too," I nodded back at Dante, then turned on my heel and started striding towards the man with the carriage. What had Gabriel said his name was? Mister Wright?

I blinked rapidly, trying to convince the tears behind my eyes to stay there, or in fact, bugger all the way off. I swallowed twice, and kept the smile on my face.

I raised my hand to the man, who was moving forward to meet me. His face brightening as I got closer.

"Cedric, thank the stars you're all right!" He called as we closed the distance between us.

"Mister Wright, is it?" I said, putting my hand out to shake it. "So sorry, I don't remember meeting you before, but jolly good of you to help out."

"Of course." He took my hand in his, his grip was firm, indeed.

"I do hope they didn't hurt you in some way," he said, looking over my shoulder where no doubt Dante and Marco had already disappeared, making their way back to the Devil's Whore. No doubt the ship was already casting off.

I didn't look back. I didn't think I could stand it. He kept his grip on my hand, and turned to open the carriage door with the other, drawing me closer to it.

"No, I'm quite all right. So, uh, I understand you've been in touch with Father?"

"Yes, of course, we can talk back at the hotel, just get up into the carriage and we'll be on our way," he said. I did as he said, stepping up into the carriage. It was confoundingly dark inside, with the curtains drawn, and I found myself quite unable to see after the bright afternoon sunlight.

Then hands grabbed me from within the carriage.

"What the devil is this?" I asked, more confused than startled, as my mind suddenly conjured images of Captain Gabriel in the dark of the carriage, stealing me back already.

I was pulled down onto the seat of the carriage and hands pulled my arms behind my back.

By this time I was less confused and more alarmed. The door to the carriage hadn't quite closed, so I thrashed my arms, trying to get loose and kicked at the shadowy figures in the dark.

"Hey! Help!" I cried out, as loudly as I could. One of my arms slipped free of my captors and I thrust it forward to push the door open. I staggered once, shoving my head out the door to shout again. "Dante!"

Then I was pulled roughly back into the carriage and the door slammed shut. Within seconds the carriage started to move, but I was still trying to fight off my unseen assailants. My arms were wrenched behind my back and I shouted again but something was stuffed into my mouth. Ropes tightened around my arms and were pulled tight, the ropes cutting into my skin.

Well, fuck.

I kicked the nearest person, my eyes were starting to adjust in the dim light, and I managed to get him between the legs, which was somewhat satisfying, even as a sense of utter dread settled over me.

"Secure his legs too, but don't hurt him, the elder won't like it if he's harmed." Hands grabbed my legs and soon they were bound as well.

I tried to ask who the fuck the elder was, but the wad of

fabric shoved into my mouth had now been secured with a scarf or something, so it just came out as noises.

"Quiet, boy." Someone lit one of the gas lamps and the interior of the carriage was brought into bright relief. I half wished it hadn't been. I was on the floor, bound and helpless, gagged and angry.

The man who had spoken leaned in, sneering unpleasantly. "Check his back, make sure it really is the right one," he said. His face was pale, pinched and dry looking. He had a very straight, pointed nose and his eyes were hooded under thick eyebrows.

Someone's hand pushed my shirt back off my shoulder.

"Aye, that's the symbol, all right. This is Cedric."

Fuck, fuck, double fuck. I'm so absolutely dead. The cult has got me, and I couldn't get away and now they have me tied up and they're going to kill me.

I hoped that Dante and Marco had somehow heard my cries for help, but my heart sank. Gabriel had got what he wanted, he'd been paid. Gabriel and his crew had no reason to care what happened to me now... unless ... they actually did like me?

But how likely is that, really? You're alone. Alone with the cult who want to kill you.

And there's nothing you can do about it.

CHAPTER 23

IN WHICH CEDRIC MEETS ELDER HARROW

The carriage ride was interminably long and rough. I couldn't move, because if I shifted even a tiny bit away from the back of the seat, I was going to fall on the floor of the carriage.

There was the creepy faced man sitting opposite me, looking at me with supreme self-satisfaction and smiling in a way that made my skin crawl.

When I craned my head to look at the others, there were three of them. One was a woman, with arched eyebrows and a modest black dress on. The other two were men, and they all looked rather pleased with themselves as well.

They didn't speak at all over the course of the ride, which was damned unsettling.

I gave up on trying to talk, there was no way I could make myself understood, and besides they weren't speaking to me or to each other. My mouth tasted of linen and my shoulders began to ache with the unnatural strain the tight ropes had put on them.

. . .

Finally, the carriage came to a stop and the woman with the eyebrows opened the door. With some difficulty I was bundled out of the carriage by the rest of them. For all the 'don't hurt him' talk, they certainly seemed happy enough to whack my shoulder on the door of the carriage and all but drop me on the ground.

We were outside some kind of estate house, not at all unlike the houses in the English countryside just out of London.

Clearly some English lord or other had brought a great deal of money to Morocco to recreate his house back home. What an expense.

We stopped directly in front of it, and I got a good look at it as I was carried in by the two men.

They took me to a side room off the foyer, and set me down on the floor.

"Ought we to remove the gag?" the woman said, and one of the men shook his head. When he replied he did so with a Spanish accent.

"Elder Harrow will do it, if he sees the need."

"I'll tell him the boy is here," the man with the pinched, pale face said.

I'm sure he heard the carriage arrive, I thought, dryly.

I squirmed into an upright position against the nearest bit of furniture, which looked to be an ornately carved and decorated wooden seat in the local style. Utterly at odds with the English manor decor.

The woman sat near me, but not close enough to touch, on the seat.

"How pretty you are," she murmured, and I wasn't sure if she intended for me to hear or was just speaking to herself. "How lucky you are, to be part of what is to come."

I turned my head enough to see her, so that I could give her an eye roll and my most skeptical arch of the brow.

There was the clatter of shoes in the hallway and a man entered the room.

The woman stood and sort of bowed to him, so I gathered he was the elder of the cult. I eyed him for any sign of ritual knife or some indication that he was about to cut my throat, but he appeared to be an ordinary man.

"Cedric Hale-Harrington, at last," he said. His accent was pure London high society, as I had guessed from the house. "Welcome to my home."

I narrowed my eyes at him, and then tossed my curls to show him how little I cared for the house.

"Natalia, would you remove the gag, I'd rather like to hear our chosen one's voice," he said. The woman smiled and knelt beside me. She slid her thumbnail along my cheek above the gag, not enough to scratch but enough that I could feel it. I didn't bother to suppress the shudder.

She gave a soft little giggle and then tugged at the knot in the back of my head, making the gag cut deeper into my mouth as she untied it.

I spat the piece of fabric out as soon as I was able. It appeared to be someone's handkerchief, now rather sodden with my spit.

She picked it up delicately and rose with a rustling of skirts. She took both scraps of material to elder Harrow.

"Thank you, dear sister. You may place these in the Great Room, next to the other artefacts. Close the door behind you, I wish to speak with him alone."

Natalia and the men skulked out, all weird and silently, and closed the door, leaving me at the foot of this cult master.

I smacked my lips, trying to stir up some moisture since the gag had taken it all away from me.

"I don't believe we've been introduced," I said, as sarcastically dry as I could manage, which wasn't easy since I was tied up on his floor. But I felt like I mustered a certain amount of irony.

"Of course. I'm elder Harrow, a member of the organisation

behind the Hellfire club, which you were so generous to attend in Kingston."

"Organisation? You mean creepy death cult," I said.

"You might see it that way," he said. He strode slowly up the room, and then back, inviting me to look at him in all his glory. "But the order of the Unknowable Way is much, much more than you think it is. And you shall be the star at the centre of it all."

I huffed and tried to find a comfortable position, which was impossible. "The last time I was kidnapped, the ropes were actually rather comfortable, your people could learn a thing or two from Captain Lucifer and his crew," I said, as if I were giving a poor report of dinner at a restaurant.

"Captain Lucifer," Harrow spat on the floor. "Interfering with our plans. We could have completed the ritual weeks ago, but he stole you out from under our noses. He and his ship will burn, mark my words."

"I will not."

"You are integral to our grand design, did you realise?"

"You put a gigantic tattoo on my back, so yes, I was *slightly* aware," I said. I tried to roll my shoulders forward to alleviate some of the strain but the ropes cut in tighter.

"Mm, yes, the tattoo. I should like to see that." He moved closer as if to touch my shoulder and seized by the annoyance of the whole thing, and no small dose of fear, I tried to bite his hand. He drew it back too quickly for me.

"Hmm, well. I'll see it in the ritual. I'll call the acolytes in to prepare you and then we'll bring you to the Great Room."

My heart thumped, and my stomach tied itself in a knot. "This ritual, I don't suppose it's a little chanting, maybe light some candles, and that's all, is it?"

Harrow smiled in a deeply unpleasant way, showing all his teeth.

"There will be candles and chanting, but there's a great deal more to it than that, chosen one. You'll play your part, whether you desire to or not. Now, you'll need to be bathed and dressed."

He turned back to the door and I kicked my bound legs uselessly. "I don't consent to being bathed by any of your bizarre cult," I said, loudly. "I don't consent to any of this!"

Harrow ignored me and called the others in.

"If I'm the chosen one like you keep on calling me, why do my desires not matter?" I asked. The Spanish sounding man hauled me to my feet.

"Because you were chosen by us, to be the vessel and the centre of it all. But we could just as easily have chosen another."

"What is that supposed to mean?" I asked, trying not to topple over, as my centre of gravity was all messed up. The Spanish man caught my arm with his hand and steadied me.

"Will you cooperate if we untie your legs?" The pinched face man asked.

"I couldn't possibly speculate," I said.

"Giuseppe, Charles. Bathe him, apply the sacred oils and dress him for the ritual," Harrow said. "I shall prepare the ritual in my own way, and we'll be ready to go when the moon sets."

CHAPTER 24

IN WHICH CEDRIC ENJOYS A BATH

he bathing wasn't nearly as bad as I'd feared it might be. For one thing, they had to untie me to do it, so my shoulders got to relax and I was able to stand unaided.

They'd brought me to what had to be the guest bedroom, which had a large porcelain tub set in the tiled antechamber. The water was steaming and pleasantly scented, and once I saw it I became utterly aware of how long it had been since I'd had a proper wash. As soon as the ropes were gone, I'd shed my clothes and jumped in without prompting, forgetting the circumstances in my need to wash the grime and sea salt off my skin.

Once I was submerged in the water, I felt my every care only distantly, so soothing was the heat on every part of me. I leaned my head back on the edge of the tub and sighed.

I heard someone clearing their throat and remembered a little of why I was there.

How best to play this? They want a frightened hostage, or a chosen one, I suppose. Well, they know I'm not going to show them how frightened I am, so I might as well play up the Chosen One aspect and see if I can't get some benefit before they do whatever awful thing the ritual entails.

Maybe if I can get them running about on errands for me, I could see a way to escape?

Unfortunately, they'd brought me upstairs, which did make the idea of escape a little more complicated, but it wasn't like I didn't have experience sneaking out of Manor houses.

I cracked open one eye.

"So, what should I be calling you two?" I asked, trying to sound like a bored prince, and not the confused captive.

"We are but humble acolytes of the Unknowable Way," Pinched Face said.

"You must have names," I prompted. "Go on, you can call me Cedric and I can call you…"

"Giuseppe," said the Spaniard. "And this is Charles."

"And how long have you been with the Unknowables?" I asked, picking up a bar of soap and making good work of scrubbing my feet.

"All my life," said Charles. "My father was Unknowable before me, and now I am lucky enough to be present as we part the stars."

I froze, remembering the stars in my dream, and what was behind them. It sounded as if Dante really had been right and they were about to try and summon some kind of ancient god from beyond, or behind, the stars.

I slipped my feet back under the water and sat more upright, washing the rest of my body slowly. My witch's charm swung and thudded dully on my chest. I hoped they hadn't noticed, I was surprised they hadn't taken it off me but perhaps they didn't know what it was.

"We ought to clean your back," Giuseppe said, almost reverently. "The symbol, it ought to be distinct, as unclouded as possible."

I inhaled and sighed out my breath. "It's fine how it is, thank you, kindly."

Giuseppe had moved closer, and was looking hopeful, smiling slightly. "I'd be happy to assist."

I stood up abruptly, the idea of this man touching my skin was abhorrent.

"That will not be necessary. Neither of you should touch me any more than you already have, it might... sully the ritual."

"We shall need to touch you in order to anoint you," Charles said.

"Charles. Charlie. Give me the oil and I'll take care of it." I held my hand out, palm up. "But you'll have to leave me alone to do it. I need some time to prepare for what's about to happen, and I can't have you two peering at me the entire time."

They exchanged looks, clearly fearful.

"If we just waited right outside the door..."

"There's nowhere he could go."

"And we'd hear him moving about even if he tried something..."

I was reminded of the two clowns I'd seen in a particularly farcical play back in London, once. I sighed, and tried to be patient as they discussed their plan. I rinsed the suds off my body and sunk under the water to rinse my hair, and they were still talking when I resurfaced.

I picked up the linen towel they'd left for me and started to dry myself off.

Finally, they agreed it could do no harm, Charles gave me the oil and they both retreated to the hallway, closing the door of the main room behind them.

I stepped out of the tub and looked around the room. My old clothes had been removed, presumably one of them were holding them out in the hall, and the only garment I could see was a pale cotton robe. I didn't like the look of that at all, but at least it would cover more than the towel. I slipped it on like a dressing gown, leaving it hanging open as apparently it had no belt. I made my way to the window and tried to get it open.

It was stiff, and I really had to yank at it before it so much as budged.

"When was the last time someone aired out this room?" I muttered, puffing out air as I strained against the stiff windowpane. Finally it slid up, but it did so with a horrible, grating screech.

"What was that noise?"

Damn it all, why did this have to be so difficult?

I shoved it up further, and was halfway out when Charles and Giuseppe burst into the room. I was trying to slip out the window when they grabbed me by my back foot and hauled me inside again.

"Though you had us fooled, didn't you?" Charles said, wrapping his arm around my waist and pulling me deeper into the room.

"Oh get off!" I cried, and stamped my heel down on the arch of his foot.

He cried out, and his grip on me loosened and I tried for the door, but Giuseppe was blocking the way.

"Now, now, quiet down," he said. "There's nowhere you can go, the house is full of Unknowables, and we all want you for the ritual."

He grabbed me by the shoulders, and my stomach turned over. The sick feeling got worse as he turned me around, stripped the robe off, letting it fall to the floor. Charles went about the oiling process. Thankfully it wasn't particularly extensive, just a few dabs of the stuff on my chest, shoulders and cheeks, and then they turned me around to smear some over the tattoo.

To my abject horror, I felt a tightening of the skin over my back.

"What is that?" I croaked. Giuseppe was holding my arms and facing me, and his face contorted with confusion.

"It stirs," Charles said. "Just as it should. You're almost

ready."

The sensation was bizarre, a tightening and releasing of my skin, moving quite without my input.

My chest tightened and I found it hard to catch my breath. My knees threatened to give out and I found myself leaning on Giuseppe. "Please, I don't want this," I gasped.

Giuseppe held me tight and Charles picked the robe back up. "Lift his arms," he said.

Giuseppe and Charles manipulated my body and slipped my arms through the robe. Some part of my mind noticed that I'd put it on backwards earlier.

The robe opened in the rear, my back exposed to the air. Charles tied something around my waist, holding it closed and hiding my buttocks. The front of it was like a seamless shirt, and was rather modest. It stuck unpleasantly to the oil on my chest.

"Don't want this, please. I'll get you money," I said, meeting Giuseppe's eyes. "If you let me go, my father will pay you so much money, I promise."

Giuseppe smiled at me as if I was an imbecile. "I don't care about money, Chosen one. I want to see what happens. I want to greet our God. I want to see the stars dance."

At his words I felt an odd twisting sensation on my back.

Did the tattoo just respond to his words? Oh fuck, I'm so fucked. I'm going to die tonight.

"Incredible," Charles said.

"We're ready. Now, Chosen One, are you going to go along nicely with us or shall we bind your hands again?"

I swallowed. I wasn't at all sure I could stand unaided, let alone walk calmly down to the room where I was going to be executed or whatever they were going to do. I swallowed the lump in my throat and tried to crack a joke.

"At least buy me dinner first."

"Tie his hands," Giuseppe said. He pulled my arms to the front and Charles produced some rope from somewhere. Had he brought it from downstairs? Was it part of the furnishings of the room? My mind spun with possibilities, fixating on this instead of what was about to happen.

The rope wound several times around my wrists and was knotted tightly.

"And I'm taking this," Giuseppe said, yanking the witch's charm off my neck, tearing the ribbon.

"Hey, no, that's mine," I said, trying uselessly to pull free of the ropes.

"Don't want outside magic interfering with the ritual." Charles said.

Then they frogmarched me downstairs.

CHAPTER 25

IN WHICH A RITUAL IS HELD

*I*t was damned uncomfortable on the table.

Giuseppe and Charles hadn't been gentle at all with the whole getting me onto the table fiasco, and to my credit, I'd fought them like a tiger. Or at least, like a scrappy house cat who didn't want to go on the table. They had overpowered me very easily after all, but I got in some good scratches before they stretched me out and tied my limbs so I could barely wriggle.

There was no good place to hold my head and my cheek had started to ache.

At least whatever had been happening on my back seemed to have stopped, although I didn't think for a moment *that* was over.

It was awful, feeling all helpless and exposed and everyone around who wanted something abhorrent. I still didn't know exactly what was going to happen, but from what I could see from the odd angle I was on, all of them had wickedly sharp blades.

Harrow approached, took up position near my head and gloated down at me. "Comfortable now are you?"

"Fuck you, you pompous, delusional jackass," I said, and I thought that was rather eloquent given the circumstances.

He rubbed his hand through my hair and chuckled. "Your part is about to begin, Chosen one. If you don't stay quiet, then I'll happily gag you again."

I tried to spit at him, but the angle was all wrong and I ended up making the table a bit wetter. Aside from that I went quiet, but only because he'd taken all the rest of my freedom and I wanted at least my tongue to deliver a witty barb at the correct sort of time.

Various people gathered around, I could hear the shuffling of their feet. After a pregnant pause, Harrow began to speak.

I hadn't been present for a lot of magic being worked, and I wasn't at all sure what to expect from it all. But as he spoke, and the others started to intone responses, I felt my attention waver. It was a little like being a few too many wines into a good party. My vision went blurry, and I blinked a few times.

Then every atom in my being was focused on the skin of my back.

The tightness I'd felt earlier was nothing compared to the sensation of my skin being pulled that hit me. I started to cry out, in surprise and pain. It felt as if there were needles in my skin, or fish hooks, drawing up towards the ceiling.

I started to gain some volume, when someone, Harrow I assumed, fisted their hand in my hair, yanked my head back and shoved a hard wooden stick into my mouth like a horse's bit.

Some part of me was grateful, I could bite down on that and it relieved a little of the pain. I closed my eyes tight and breathed hard as the pain died off and I was washed with a feeling of numbness. Whatever had happened on my back had subsided to something like movement without the pain.

Perhaps it's someone with a paintbrush, making a landscape on my skin. Or perhaps it's a seascape, with a beautiful ship on it?

That thought made me tear up, although I wasn't sure why.

I faded in and out of a dreamlike state, aware of little except for the sounds of voices and an ongoing creeping sensation on my back.

CHAPTER 26

IN WHICH CAPTAIN LUCIFER ATTEMPTS A
RESCUE

*G*abriel swore again.

"These horses aren't nearly fast enough," he snapped.

"It's a complicated ritual," Dante said. "We have time."

"You don't know that."

"I almost fell off the horse again!" Marco called from behind them. Dante hissed beside him and leaned forward, urging his horse to run faster.

The road the carriage had taken was at least relatively smooth. Hiring the horses had cost them precious time, as had instructing the crew on how to ride. Now, Gabriel felt every second ticking past as if it were the end of the world.

What had they done to Cedric already?

How could he have been so stupid as to ignore the uncomfortable feeling in his stomach? How had he let Cedric go at all?

The road led to a large, English style manor house. The black carriage was outside, parked in the front. Gabriel smiled grimly.

"There, we have you now."

Dante held up a hand and reined his horse in, the others all pulled their horses down to a walk. "It's best if we can maintain the element of surprise," Dante said. "We have no idea how many are inside."

Gabriel nodded his assent and led the crew to the garden on the side of the road and dismounted. The horses could graze while they retrieved Cedric from inside.

Dante and a few of the rest of the men dismounted smartly, but Marco more or less fell off his horse.

He walked up to Gabriel with a pained look on his face. "That hurt, and I didn't like it. I'll come back on someone else's horse as an otter."

"Fine." Gabriel drew a dagger. He eyed the house. "One group will go in the back through the servant's entrance. I'll use the front door. Dante?"

"I'll go high," he said. Then he put his hand on Gabriel's shoulder and squeezed it. They gazed into each other's eyes for a brief moment. "We'll get him back."

"I might burn the house down," Gabriel said, trying to control the anger threatening to overcome him. "If they have hurt him..."

Dante nodded as if this were something he had expected. "Try to stay quiet as long as you can, Captain."

They started walking towards the house, sticking to the shadows of the garden, although it didn't look like there was anyone keeping watch. Appearances could be deceiving, though.

Marco took a half dozen men and skirted around the back of the house.

Dante looked up at the wall and then started to scale it, finding finger and toe holds where Gabriel could see only smooth wall.

"One of the benefits of being a vampire," Gabriel murmured to himself. Then he signalled to Kaito and the remaining members of his crew and they approached the front door. Moving as silently as they could.

The door was locked, so Gabriel gestured Kaito forward. "Pick it."

Kaito nodded, withdrew his lock picks from inside his jacket and got to work. It didn't take long at all, and the door swung open silently.

Gabriel led the way, moving slowly so as to not make a sound on the floorboards.

His experience in houses such as this one gave him a good understanding of the layout of the rooms, but that didn't mean he knew where they had Cedric.

He paused a few steps in and listened, tuning out the sounds of his crew behind him.

There was movement in the room to his right. From the large double doors it looked to be a ballroom of some sort, the doors closed and unwelcoming.

There was the slightest noise on the stairway. Gabriel looked up to see Dante descending, sword in hand. He shook his head, indicating that Cedric was not on the upper level.

Shadows moved down the hallway and Marco appeared from the kitchens, the others behind him.

Gabriel nodded at the double doors and lifted his fingers to his lips.

Marco pointed to the wall near him, there was another set of doors there. Gabriel nodded and approached the door, holding his sword in guard position as he closed his hand over the door handle.

Dante was beside him in a heartbeat, his hand on the other door handle.

Their eyes met. Gabriel tipped his chin up and they threw the doors open.

The room was rather dark inside. None of the lamps were lit, instead there were candles dotted here and there. Large candles, of the kind you might see in a church, as wide as Gabriel's arm.

The flickering light made the hooded figures seem even more ominous.

Although, as a few of them turned to look at the interlopers, the faces looked largely ordinary under the hoods. They seemed to be chanting something, although Gabriel couldn't make out the words.

About a score of robed people stood in a loose ring around a heavy wooden table. On the table was the familiar form of Cedric, tied spread eagled on his front, wearing a curious robe that left his back bare. Gabriel froze as his eyes traveled over the sight.

Because the tattoo seemed to be moving.

And that was surely impossible.

In the moment he hesitated, one of the cultists cried out. Her voice pierced the room. "They're trying to stop the ritual! Kill them!"

Gabriel snapped to attention, Marco had come in the other doors with the others, they were now circling around the other side.

Beside him, Dante hissed, and Gabriel knew from experience that he was baring his sharp fangs, ready to feed. Gabriel felt no pity for any who would feel the pierce of Dante's fangs tonight.

The cultists closest to Gabriel drew daggers and knives and turned to face them. "No mercy!" Gabriel cried. "Rescue Cedric!"

He rushed at the nearest two cultists, swinging his cutlass.

CHAPTER 27

IN WHICH A BATTLE IS LOST AND WON

*T*here was something wrong.

I knew a little then, what was supposed to be happening. It was the thing on my back. The chanting was waking it up.

The chanting was delightfully discordant, hurting my ears like the ringing of an incessant bell while a child banged on a drum at random. But the discordant pain was correct, somehow.

Something had interrupted it, and the pain was at the edge of my consciousness, waiting to strike again. I thought perhaps if the chant was more constant the pain would stay away.

The chanting was accentuated by some other voices. They were cutting through the discordance. I inhaled as deeply as I could through my nose. There was something in my mouth, and my jaw ached from clenching down on it, so much that I couldn't let go of it.

I gave up on that, and tried to open my eyes instead.

The room was bright, glaring, and my eyelids fluttered.

A voice cut through my blurry mind. It was a voice I knew. A voice I really liked. Who was that?

"Cut him free!"

I saw the flash of a blade, and the tension on my left wrist eased. Gratefully, I curled my arm towards me. My back ached still, but something didn't seem as directly dangerous as it had been.

In a moment my right wrist was released as well, and then my legs. I curled on my side and sighed with relief, the thing in my mouth fell out as well and I smiled a little at the relief that washed over me.

"All right, Cedric?" I opened my eyes to see Gabriel. In his glorious, impressive garb as Captain Lucifer. I wasn't at all sure he was really there, but I was happy to see him all the same.

"Hello?" I said, and my voice sounded very far away indeed.

"Get back, Captain Lucifer, you foul dog!" That was Harrow's voice. I tried to sit up but my head spun and something behind my eyes throbbed, I crumpled back onto my elbows and watched helplessly as Harrow went for Gabriel with a dagger raised overhead.

Gabriel brought his cutlass up with a swift movement that my blurry eyes could hardly follow. There was the ringing sound of steel on steel and it stuck in my ears like a whining gnat that wouldn't fade away.

"Some cheek you have, calling me foul, when you were about to sacrifice this boy for your own means," Gabriel hissed, and wrenched Harrow's weapon from his hand.

"He chose it," Harrow said, his voice going deeper in tone. "He came to us and begged for deliverance."

My mind was clouded, but even still I was relatively sure that wasn't the case. "Don't think so..." I managed to grate out.

They ignored me.

Harrow backed away from Gabriel and his cutlass, and they were still arguing but I couldn't exactly follow the words they were saying. I had to get my head back together, somehow. I wondered if anyone had any coffee.

I turned my head slowly, looking around the room. There

were hooded figures, battling pirates. The pirates were cutting people down, one of the candles had been knocked over.

My stomach lurched, nausea surged and my back stung as if whipped with a birch rod. I cried out as loudly as I could manage without vomiting.

I heard a cry, which felt like it was responding to my cry of agony. Then strong hands seized my hips and pulled me off the table.

"There now, I've got you Cedric, you're quite safe," a deep and familiar voice murmured.

My vision had gone blurry from the intensity of the pain but it cleared as the strong hands bore me up. I blinked until I could see Dante's face, his fangs were out and there was a drop of blood in the corner of his mouth.

"You came for me," I whispered.

"Of course I did."

"My back..." my words died in my throat, explaining it all seemed beyond me.

He wrapped his arm around my waist and pulled me close against him, drew his sword with his other hand and skewered one of the cultists. Blood sprayed impressively into the air, and I got quite distracted watching the scarlet sheet of viscous fluid. The way the candlelight caught the colour was really quite beautiful.

Dante tensed and inhaled the scent, then, shoving me behind him he fell on the body and fed.

It was, I thought vaguely, rather horrifying to watch him like this.

I directed my eyes elsewhere in the room. Gabriel had Harrow backed against the table, the point of his cutlass under his chin. Harrow still seemed to be talking, which beggared belief.

Marco and Kaito were fighting together, side by side and cutting through hooded figures with ease. It certainly seemed as if the pirates were winning, and easily too, which was definitely a relief.

They came to rescue me. Gabriel cares, Dante cares. They all want me to be safe! I let myself feel a little thrill of excitement.

A hand gripped my wrist, which was sore from the ropes and I winced.

"That's it, Chosen One, come with me now and we can still salvage the ritual," a woman's voice said. I turned to look at Natalia. She drew me back, away from Dante, which wasn't what I wanted at all.

"No, not that." I pulled against her hold on me but I didn't feel as strong as normal.

"It's all right, pretty, lets go."

Had they drugged me somehow? Was there something in the oil perhaps? Or maybe it was simply the magic and my tattoo.

I bit my tongue in the hopes that the pain would clear my mind, and then I sucked in the biggest breath I could manage.

"Cedric!" That was Dante. Natalia pulled me close against her chest and brought her knife to my throat. My back stung everywhere it touched her and I whimpered with the pain of it.

I blinked, feeling my senses return at this sudden and very immediate threat to my life.

"Don't you harm him," Dante said. He leaned forward, his shoulders forward, his sword raised and his other hand before him in a quelling gesture. "If you cut his skin I swear I will make you suffer."

"Oh, you're a vampire," Natalia said, she was moving, pulling me back towards the door. "How fascinating. We could offer you so much, you know. The Unknowable Way would treat you like a king. You could have the boy, even, as long as you let us do the ritual. You could have everything you wanted."

I lifted my leg to try and stamp on her foot but she'd pulled me off balance enough that I couldn't get any traction, and stumbled forward, grazing my throat on the knife. Just another thread of pain through my body. I whimpered louder.

Dante's eyes fixed on my neck and his pupils expanded, slitting in the middle like a cat's eyes. His mouth dropped open and his sword hand wavered.

"That's right," Natalia hauled me upright again. "You want him? You want his blood? You can have it, just come with me."

We were almost at the door now.

"Sister!" I heard Harrow call from the table. "What are you-"

The voice cut off into a gurgle, and I imagined Gabriel had cut his throat but I didn't dare look away from Dante. In my ear I heard Natalia whisper "Rupert," in a pained way. Her grip on me tightened.

"Dante, focus," I rasped. "It's me, you said you wouldn't... you said I was safe with you, remember?"

Dante's eyes flicked to my eyes and seemed to become a little more human.

He snarled and lunged forward, thrusting with his rapier. Natalia pulled the knife away from my throat and wrapped her arm around my neck instead, still trying to get away. But Dante's aim had been true and she collapsed, with me on top of her.

She was gasping and twitching and her grip on me had loosened so I rolled away, cursing as the robe got caught under her.

"Fucking, fuck..." I yanked at the robe and it tore, revealing more of my legs. Dante offered me his hand and pulled me to my feet.

He exhaled slowly and nodded once at me. "Are you all right?"

"No," I said. My hands found his chest and I leaned my weight on him. "I am most distinctly not all right and I'd like to go back to the ship now, please."

A body fell nearby and Gabriel appeared beside Dante. "All right?"

"More or less," Dante said. "He's asking to go back to the ship."

"I think that's a fine idea." Gabriel ruffled my hair and then looked around the room. "A few ran for it. I think the wall is on fire judging from the smoke. Anything worth stealing in this place?"

I shook my head. "No idea, Harrow must have money but..."

Gabriel nodded. "Back to the horses! Grab anything that looks valuable!"

"What happened to Harrow?" I asked, suddenly needing to know for sure that he was gone from the world.

"The leader? Dead," Gabriel said. He nodded at me. "You don't have to fear him anymore."

Dante wrapped his arm around me and took some of my weight. I glanced behind to see Natalia's body but there was nothing there but a pool of blood. "Natalia? She's gone..."

Dante glanced over and huffed his breath out. "Never mind, let's get you out of here before the smoke fills the room."

I didn't argue with that.

CHAPTER 28

IN WHICH THERE IS A DEEPLY
UNCOMFORTABLE HORSE RIDE

The ride back to the ship was deeply unpleasant. Once we were out in the cool night air, I realised how little protection from the elements the thin linen robe offered. I shivered against Dante's side.

One good thing was that the tattoo on my back seemed to have stopped moving. Whether it was the chanting, or enough of the oil had been rubbed off in the scuffle with Natalia, I had no idea.

The crew slowly assembled out the front, where there were a flock of horses milling about eating the rose bushes. There were people leaving the house who I didn't recognise, but guessed from their garb that they were servants. Marco walked out, in conversation with a chambermaid. She had an armful of fine silk dresses, and the two of them were laughing.

"It appears there's no loyalty to the cult among the servants," Marco said, as he ambled over to Gabriel, a handful of gold jewellery in his fist. "Andrea there assures me that there were never any pirates here, and their master died hosting a wild party that got out of hand."

"Excellent news."

I shuddered extra hard against Dante's side.

Gabriel took one look at me shivering, shrugged off his black coat and draped it around my shoulders as Dante let go of me. It was an instant relief. I had assumed that the fabric hitting my abused back would smart but it simply felt warm and soft. I slipped my arms into the sleeves and wrapped it around me. At least three sizes too big, but it smelled like Gabriel. Gunpowder, sweat and the salt of the sea.

"Come on, Cedric, you can ride with me," he said. Dante shot him a look, and Gabriel waved his hand.

"There's blood on his throat, I don't want you getting distracted, Dante. The house is burning and we need to be well clear before anyone else turns up." Gabriel offered his hand to me and I took it, glancing at Dante apologetically.

"There is unfinished business," Dante said.

"We'll talk in my cabin," Gabriel said, his tone becoming impatient. He lifted me by the waist and I had to scramble to get my leg over the horse. Damned uncomfortable it was too, as I had nothing like riding gear on.

Gabriel held me with one arm as he led the pirates back to the ship. They were not all natural equestrians.

But I was largely distracted from the amusing sight of Marco trying to stay in the saddle because I was in so damned much physical distress. I had to try and wad up the remaining bits of torn robe between my legs, which offered some protection at least, but that left my bare legs rubbing against the side of the horse, which wasn't at all downy and soft.

Then there was the sting in my ankles and wrists from the harsh ropes that had lashed me to the table, and actually, now that I had the time to think about it, all my pre-bath aches in my shoulders and back had returned as well.

On top of all of that my throat had literally been cut. Not enough to endanger my life and, when I felt gingerly at it with my fingertips, I could tell it had stopped bleeding, but it still bloody well hurt. I could have died!

Gabriel's strong arm kept me pressed against his chest and his warmth and solidarity behind me was a comfort, at least.

Finally the docks came into view and I felt a certain amount of tension leave my chest. I began to shake again and pulled Gabriel's coat closer around me.

Gabriel pulled his horse up near to the ship.

"Can you get down all right?" He murmured in my ear. In all truth, I probably could have tried, but I was feeling far too sorry for myself to admit it. I liked the way he'd been holding me too much. I shook my head.

"I don't think so."

"All right, hold on and I'll lift you down," he said.

I gripped the saddlehorn and steadied myself as Gabriel swung down elegantly off the horse. I really had to ask him about his past one of these days, as it seemed he'd had a lot of practise in the saddle.

He lifted me down as if I weighed nothing, and set me on my feet. "All right?"

I had half been pretending I couldn't manage, but after the horse ride my legs were quite sore, and my body felt very tired indeed.

I gripped his arm. "Not quite as steady as I could be."

"Hmm." He bent and scooped me up in his arms. I gratefully put my arms around his neck.

"I'll make sure the horses are returned to the stable," Kaito said, and took the reins of Gabriel's horse.

"Thank you, Kaito. Everyone else, back to the ship and cast off. I want to be well clear of Casablanca in the next hour. Dante, a word in my cabin."

With that, Gabriel carried me onto the ship, into his cabin and laid me down gently on his bed. Dante was close behind us, and closed the door behind him, then went around the room lighting the lamps.

Outside I could hear the shouts of preparation to leave,

unfurling the sails and so on. It was a funny time of night to be leaving but I did agree with Gabriel that it would be good to leave as soon as possible. I settled myself on the bed, tugging at the skirt of the robe, which was determined to ride up scandalously. I had no reason at all to feel shy, except that Gabriel was looking me over, scrutinising me. I felt rather exposed.

He sat on the bed beside me and he picked up my hand to examine my wrist, frowning deeply at the abrasion there.

"Dante, if you wouldn't mind, there's a salve in the third drawer by the door. Brown clay pot, would you bring it here?"

"Of course." Dante brought the small clay pot to him, and Gabriel opened it, dipped his finger in and then spread the salve over the marks on my wrist. It numbed it a little, and then warmed gently. I sighed in relief as one of the pains in my body vanished.

To my own surprise, I felt tears well up in my chest. I swallowed the lump in my throat, and then swallowed again.

Dante took a little salve, sat on the other side of me and started rubbing it into my other wrist.

The simple fact of the two of them looking after me, of being gentle and kind, it brought home just how much danger I had been in. I'm not at all sure why, since I was safe now, I knew that, but I was overcome with emotion.

I nearly died.

My breath caught in my chest and tears slipped out of my eyes. I tugged my hand back from Gabriel and dabbed at my eyes with the sleeve of his coat.

"It's all right," Dante said. "You're safe."

I looked at Gabriel, biting my lip.

The ship moved, a swelling under us, and I knew we'd cast off from Casablanca and had truly left the cult behind. The cult who had been largely killed, anyway. The cult the pirates had saved me from.

Gabriel's lips turned into a frown and his eyebrows pulled together, the picture of sympathy. "I'm so sorry, Cedric," he said. "I should have been more careful. You shouldn't have had to go through any of that."

I started blubbering. The fear and the relief overwhelmed me. I covered my face with my hands and curled in on myself.

I felt Dante move behind me, getting closer, putting his arms around me. "It's all right. We won't let them anywhere near you again."

The sobbing lasted perhaps a minute before I felt a little less dreadful. Pressing myself against Dante's chest helped, and I felt Gabriel's hand on my thigh, his thumb rubbing gentle circles into my skin.

Finally, I thought I could speak without crying, so I dropped my hands from my face and sniffed. Gabriel smiled softly at me and reached for my foot. I pulled them up onto the bed and he gently and quietly rubbed salve on the marks on my ankles.

It was incredibly sweet of him.

"Thank you," I said, my voice a little watery.

"Of course."

"Is there something, uh, that could clean the oil off my back?" I asked.

Dante found a rag, pulled the coat off my shoulders and gently wiped at my skin. Nothing had moved on there since the Manor house but it felt better to know the oil was cleaned. He pulled the coat back on, presumably because I was still shivering a little. And then his arms were around me again and I felt almost content.

Gabriel finished gently rubbing my ankles, and left one hand on my leg as he straightened up to look at me, wrapped in his coat and then in his quartermaster.

"I suppose we ought to talk about what happens next," Dante said, slowly. His grip tightened on me, just a bit.

"I don't wish to get in between the two of you," Gabriel said, slowly, although his thumb was still rubbing my skin.

My heart sped up just a little as Dante inhaled. "I don't think it's... you had the prior claim," Dante said. "And you're captain."

"I'm not choosing between the two of you," I said quickly. "I like you both, I *want* you both. And I have had fantasies about all three of us, if that's something ... the both of you might be into." I could hardly believe I was brave enough to be suggesting this now, but after nearly dying and all that, it didn't seem like such a big deal. "I want you both." I said again.

Gabriel raised an eyebrow and the corner of his mouth twitched up. "Dante? Is that something you would be interested in as well?"

Dante nodded, I felt his cheek move against my head. "Yes, Captain. Ever since... well, we met, yes. But since Cedric told me about... what he imagined, with the three of us. I have had trouble ridding my mind of the idea."

"I've often wished I could bend you over my knee and spank you when you anger me," Gabriel said, his smile perfectly wicked. I squirmed, feeling myself get hard at the thought of Gabriel disciplining Dante in such a way.

"Much as I wish to try all manner of rough and scandalous things with the both of you, at once," I said, slowly, half regretting the words I was about to speak, because they were so sensible, but I had just cried in front of them both. "I rather think tonight I might need gentler treatment."

"Of course," Gabriel leaned in and kissed me, gently and tenderly. I felt something sweet from his kiss, something like his apology, and his regret and his desire to have me in his arms. I sighed into his mouth. He pulled back a little, flicked his eyes to Dante and kissed him over my shoulder. Being pressed in between the two of them had me hard as a rock instantly, and I tentatively brought a hand up to touch Gabriel's chest.

Dante made a noise of such need and yearning that I echoed

it without thinking. Gabriel sat back, Dante let go of me and the two of them pulled the coat back off my shoulders and Dante got up to set it aside.

Gabriel pulled on the cult's robe and it slipped off me easily. I lay back on my elbows, breathing heavily. He stood and caught Dante on his way back to the bed, kissing him soundly and pulling his shirt open.

Dante's hands went to the waistband of Gabriel's trousers and they were stripping each other, kissing and panting as they worked.

Once they were both naked, Gabriel gripped Dante by the back of the neck and turned to look at me. "How do you feel about me fucking Cedric while he fucks you? Gently and slowly, of course."

He said it so casually he might have been suggesting who takes first watch, but the words were so loaded with desire, and the room was so charged with it, that I held my breath.

Dante nodded, rested his forehead against Gabriel's and groaned softly. "May I feed?"

Gabriel smiled, but there was a cold edge to it, I recognised the look from when he had me shackled to the bed. My skin prickled with excited anticipation.

"Ask your captain politely, and then we'll see."

Dante straightened up, blushing ever so slightly and looked Gabriel in the eyes. "May I please feed, Captain?"

Gabriel's eyes grew brighter and he nodded. "You may, on Cedric or myself."

Dante's tongue flicked out to wet his lips in a quick movement, and I shifted on the bed, reaching my hands out to them. "Come *on* then."

"Still impatient, even now..." Gabriel smiled and shook his head. "I really am going to have to teach you to wait. But not tonight. Tonight, I'm just glad you're alive."

With those unexpected words, he wrapped his arm around

my waist and kissed me with abandon, the kind of kiss that promised a great deal of fun. I returned it with interest, my other hand still reaching for Dante, who caught it and kissed the tips of my fingers. Then the bed shifted as he climbed in behind me again, his lips kissing their way up my arm and to my shoulder.

I moaned softly, yearning for more even as I was being given exactly what I wanted.

Gabriel moved between my legs, his hand sliding slowly up my thigh with an exquisitely teasing movement. Dante set the pot of oil before me, and Gabriel slicked his fingers with it before starting to work me open.

I leaned back into Dante, resting my head on his shoulder and tipping my chin up for a kiss from him. He obliged me instantly, and I felt again that strange bond between us, the ineffable connection that had been sealed when he fed off me.

My cock was throbbing with need, and as if he could tell, Gabriel dipped his head down to lick at the head of it as his fingers delved deeper inside, stretching me with practised ease. I was quickly getting impatient for more, but I realised that if I were to be having my way with Dante I ought to be preparing him as well...

I twisted a little and Dante stroked his hand through my hair. "What are you trying to do, sunshine?"

I smiled, hearing his nickname for me, and kissed his chin, my torso twisting to see him. "Get you ready for me, of course."

Gabriel twisted his fingers inside me, hitting that glorious spot and making me cry out, at the same time he dropped his mouth down over me and my eyes fluttered shut, moaning.

"Mm, distracted, I see," Dante said. He kissed my mouth and shifted a little, moving more to the side of me. If I'd been able to I'd have turned to him, but my bones all seemed to be made of jelly while Gabriel stroked inside me. "Have some pity, will you, Captain?"

Gabriel sat up and withdrew his fingers, wiping his mouth with his other arm. "Very well. Shall I stretch you too, Dante?"

I groaned my assent, wanting desperately to see him worked over by Gabriel.

Gabriel moved up between my legs, grinding himself against me in an entirely distracting way, as Dante let his legs fall open and smirked at the both of us. I reached to stroke his cock as Gabriel pushed his fingers, still slick from me, into Dante.

It was an intoxicating sight, heightened by the swell of emotions in my chest. Gratitude that they'd come to rescue me, the relief that I had, thus far at least, survived the night, and an intense affection for the both of them.

Those feelings could be dangerous... those last ones. Those were the feelings that could entangle my heart, tear it apart and leave it broken in pieces. I ignored them all, focusing again on the sensations I was feeling. The silky smoothness of Dante's cock in my hand, pulsing in response to my movements. Gabriel pressing his hips against my thighs, his cock sliding against mine with the most incredible drag. Dante's face contorted as he made a low keening sound. My own heart sped up at the sight of him, and Gabriel, apparently quite able to take care of multiple things at once, closed his mouth over my nipple and sucked it until it was hard.

"That's enough, I'm ready," Dante said, his voice strained. "Please..."

"Yes, please, I need more." I let go of Dante's cock to take hold of Gabriel's hips, pushing them back so I could turn over. I got to my hands and knees and Gabriel slapped my ass, although not as hard as he might have done. I gasped, and closed my eyes, the mattress moved as Gabriel lined himself up behind me and pushed inside.

"Yes, thank Go..." I caught myself and changed my choice of words. "Thank the stars. I needed this."

I lifted my arm and Dante moved beneath me, his eyes blue

as the sea on a sunny day. His expression blissful already. I licked my lips and leaned down to kiss him as his hand found my cock and stroked it gently.

I'd asked for something gentle, but I began to suspect that somehow this would still be too much for me. Gabriel gripped me by the hips to guide me down. Dante splayed his legs wide under me, and his hand led my cock to his hole. Filled utterly by Gabriel, and then pushing myself into Dante to fill him, I almost orgasmed on the spot.

Hold it back, Cedric, this is a dream come true. And a good dream, not one of the shitty cult nightmares. And who knows when it will happen again, so enjoy it.

I swallowed, leaned in, and kissed Dante as I pushed all the way inside him. Gabriel wrapped his arm around my waist and started to gently guide me, pulling himself out of me and pulling me back a little as he did, so that I withdraw partially from Dante.

Like the cusp of a wave, we all hovered for a moment on the edge of pleasure, before Gabriel shoved forward so my hips pressed into Dante's thighs and I was deep inside him and utterly filled with Gabriel at the same time.

"Ohhh stars," I groaned.

Dante leaned up to kiss at my neck, and Gabriel's mouth found the skin of my shoulder blade and bit it gently. I shivered, overwhelmed with trying to keep track of everywhere I was being touched. Trying to process all the good feelings at once.

Gabriel kissed Dante over my shoulder again, and I bucked against the both of them, forward into Dante and then back into Gabriel, feeling very gratified when they both moaned louder into their kiss.

"I won't last long," I gasped, dropping my forehead to Dante's shoulder.

"Don't try to hold it off," Gabriel said. "Just feel it all."

I did so, closing my eyes and giving over to it it. Caught

between two such handsome and desirable men, I rode the waves of desire until I was bucking and orgasming into Dante. He chose that moment to sink his teeth into the fleshy part of my shoulder, right over where Gabriel had playfully bitten earlier.

I moaned, feeling even more arousal pumping out of me in time with the blood.

Gabriel made a slightly strangled noise and shoved his hips deep inside me, filling me with his hotness and making my head spin a little.

Dante's cock twitched between us and somehow I managed to put my hand between us to stroke the orgasm out of him, too.

Gabriel's hips slowed and he carefully eased out of me. I groaned, lacking the strength to do the same, thankfully I fell his hands on his hips, guiding me with gentle force. With his assistance, I was able to roll onto my back, and lie there with my eyes closed, panting hard.

"Mmm," Gabriel said. The mattress moved as if he were leaving but in a moment he was back with a soft damp cloth, cleaning me up.

Dante wrapped an arm around me and gently licked at the wound he'd made on my shoulder, and then the one on my neck from the knife. It was so intensely intimate that my spent cock made a half-hearted attempt to get hard again.

But I was well and truly exhausted. With the release of the orgasm, I felt myself quickly slipping into a worn out sleep.

"Rest, sunshine, you've done enough for the day now," Dante murmured.

Gabriel settled on my other side, and arranged himself so my head was pillowed on his chest.

I decided to take his word for it. "Right then," I mumbled, no doubt slurring my words as I faded into blissful nothingness. "Thank you, love you."

CHAPTER 29

TEN DAYS LATER

*W*e sailed up the Thames and I felt a pang of something like fear, quickly overwhelmed by nostalgia. I leaned my arms on the side of the ship and watched as London town with all its buildings and smoke stacks resolved itself in front of me.

It was a beautiful angle for the city, and with my oils I'd be able to make a pretty picture of it. Dirt and all.

Because beauty isn't about purity, I think, it's about the thing existing as it is, flaws and all. Gabriel is beautiful and he has plenty of scars. Dante is devastatingly handsome and he's hiding such a secret. One he'd call a curse, although I'm not sure I agree.

Gabriel was dressed in his Sir Gabriel garb, looking every bit the handsome gentleman who operated a successful shipping company. He strode up the deck to stand beside me, shooting his cuffs.

"How long has it been since you saw her?" he asked.

"Her?"

"The city of London."

I tried to count the months for a moment, until I got bored. "A while." I smiled up at him. "I don't care for the temperature."

He grimaced in sympathy and patted my shoulder. As I'd

lost even the clothes I was kidnapped in, I'd been borrowing from the crew since Casablanca. For my triumphant return to London I'd borrowed one of Dante's fine linen white shirts (although it was a little long in the arms), and a waistcoat from Kaito. The trousers were Marco's, since he was more or less my size and a pair of his boots as well, although those were a little on the tight side.

"Indeed, it's nothing like as balmy as the Caribbean," Gabriel said. I watched the smile on his face for a few moments longer than I needed to and then turned my gaze back to the city.

With the ship's sails flapping white and innocent, and the name of the ship altered with a handy bit of magic Gabriel had trapped in the wooden boards of the ship, we sailed into dock as an ordinary merchantman and his law-abiding crew.

Gabriel paid the dockmaster and signed in under Sir Gabriel Durant. Together with Dante, we walked through the busy docks and into the city of London.

The uneven cobbles played havoc on my feet in the slightly too small boots and I started to become anxious to get to my parents' house if only to take the weight off my feet.

"It's just up here," I said, leading them down past Trafalgar to the small townhouse Father had bought when I was twelve years old and he'd come into some money through clever business deals.

I spotted the familiar green painted door and went to it, knocking on it several times.

I turned to look at Gabriel and Dante as I waited for one of the staff to open the door. Gabriel looked confident as ever, but Dante looked positively nervous.

The door opened, revealing a footman I didn't recognise.

"Er, hello, I'm Cedric Hale-Harrington, Ackley's son. Might be we let in?"

The footman's eyes widened and he stepped back to admit us. "Of course, young master. Please, go through to the sitting room, your father is at parliament but your mother will be overjoyed to see you, of course."

Dante hesitated at the door, and I turned. "Please come in, Dante," I said. Remembering belatedly, that he'd mentioned needing to be explicitly invited into a dwelling.

He smiled and stepped through.

It felt damned strange to wait in the sitting room, although it had been a good bit more than a year, perhaps more like two, since I was here. Perhaps I should have tried harder to remember what month it had been when I was first sent overseas...

In the sitting room, Gabriel took a seat and appeared to be at his ease. Dante stood by the unlit fireplace, looking out of place and uncomfortable. I sat on an armchair and then stood again, because now that I was almost about to see my mother I was excited and nervous.

Her soft footsteps heralded her arrival and I shoved my hand through my hair and forgot how to breathe.

She walked in and didn't even spare a glance at Gabriel or Dante. Her face split into a wide, delighted smile as she rushed towards me. I opened my arms and we embraced.

"Oh, Mother." Her gentle rosewater scent flooded me with memories and I felt warmth spread through my bones, I was so happy to see her.

"Cedric, my wayward son," she breathed into my hair. "I was so worried, so... terrified I wouldn't see you again. Oh, my boy." Her arms around me tightened and I smiled against the soft fabric of her sleeve.

Finally, we pulled back, she held me at arm's length and looked me up and down. "Was it terribly awful? What am I saying? Of course it was. You were kidnapped by that terrible pirate. Well, I'm glad you're safe back home, now."

"So am I, Mother," I gave her a kiss on the cheek and then stood back. "It's my pleasure to introduce you to Sir Gabriel

Durant, my rescuer. And this is Mister Grigorias, his quartermaster. Gentlemen, please meet my mother, Violet Hale-Harrington."

They made niceties and small talk for a while. Mother thanked the both of them, and Gabriel told her the story we'd concocted together of rescuing me in Casablanca after the vicious Captain Lucifer had sold me to some ale-house as cheap labour. It was far-fetched to be sure, but not really any more so than what had actually happened.

Mother's gratitude was profuse indeed, and she sat beside me on the sofa, her hand on mine, a soft, light presence.

"You must return for dinner and meet Ackley," she said. "Indeed, I insist upon it. He'll want to thank you himself and we must do something to demonstrate our gratitude."

"Of course, it would be our utmost pleasure," Gabriel said.

Gabriel and Dante excused themselves and promised to return later in the day. Mother hugged me again and then looked me up and down. "Oh dear, we will have to get the tailors in. I expect you've outgrown the clothes you left here. Oliver brought back a chest of your things from Kingston of course, but new things would be just the thing to cheer you, wouldn't they?"

"Oliver, yes," I said, my heart racing suddenly. "Is he here? Or..."

"He has an apartment in town," Mother said. "Your father cancelled his contract since you were obviously no longer in his charge. Oh, don't pull that face, we paid him a generous severance."

"I should very much like to see him," I said. "If you'll give me his address, I could-"

Mother held up a hand and shook her head. "No question. I've just got you back and I'm not having you wandering off by yourself to be kidnapped again. I'll have Stevens send word, he can visit for dinner as well, if you like. But you are staying within these walls for the moment."

I hoped that wasn't what she considered a permanent plan, but I was comforted to know I'd at least be seeing Oliver again soon.

"Thank you, Mother. I'll retire to my room for the moment, and get changed."

I kissed her cheek again and headed upstairs to my old bedroom, my heart thumping and my mind racing as I tried to work out what in the world I should say to Oliver.

CHAPTER 30

IN WHICH OLIVER AND CEDRIC SPEAK OF
IMPORTANT MATTERS

I was passing the time by sorting through the paints and painting supplies I still had in my old desk. Many of the paints had dried up, but there were one or two tubes that were salvageable.

I had opened my travelling trunk as well, and was pleased to see Oliver had very carefully packed all my clothes and supplies in layers of tissue paper. He'd taken a lot of care, which warmed me even as my heart ached for what it might mean. Was it possible he cared for me?

There was a knocking at the door downstairs, and I froze, wondering if it were Gabriel and Dante back already, although it was still early for dinner...

I heard a familiar voice, and the sound of footsteps, flying up the stairs.

The door to my room, which I'd left slightly ajar, slammed open and there was Oliver. His face flushed as if he'd been running.

"You're all right!" He exclaimed.

My heart swelled at the enthusiasm he seemed to be showing, but I averted my eyes as I carefully set down the tube of burnt Sienna. What I had to say to him wasn't going to be at all easy, but it must be done.

I swallowed, summoned up my courage and turned to face him. "Yes, I'm quite well, all in one piece."

He closed the distance between us with two strides and wrapped me in a bear hug, which was highly unexpected, but very welcome indeed. I hugged him back gratefully and allowed myself a glimmer of hope, squeezing him against me a little more than was strictly platonic.

"Oliver, it's so very good to see you, incredible, really, but we need to talk."

He pulled back and gave me the severe look I'd come to associate with him asking me to practice my Latin. "We do?"

"Yes, would you like to sit?"

I gestured to one of the chairs in my room, which had customarily been draped with clothes, but was for the moment clear and tidy. He sat down and folded his hands in front of him.

I sat opposite him, on the bed, which felt a little intimate but, well. He'd come to my bedroom. He'd seen me blind drunk and in danger of pissing myself, he could take it.

"So, well, you see, the fact of it is," I started. Then I heard myself dithering and just blurted out the important bits, instead. "I've been desperately in love with you for a long time, Oliver. I mean, I know you knew I was partial to lovers of all sexes, but it was you who I actually pined for." I swallowed and looked at his face. He seemed to have frozen, so I plowed on. "And well, I was kidnapped by pirates and they were not as scary as they should have been, and I ... yes, well, I dallied with them. And that's not because I stopped wanting you, but I did think of you and I had no idea if you felt anything similar to me at all."

I paused for breath.

Oliver cleared his throat. "Cedric..." he trailed off again, looking away. His eyes were obscured a little by the reflection of light off his glasses.

Now that would be interesting to paint.

By the stars, Cedric, not the time.

"The fact is," I said, to break the silence. "The fact is I still feel that way about you, and I intend to get permission from my father to go back to sea with Sir Gabriel, who ... who rescued me from Casablanca, and I would very much like it if you'd consider joining me. I could pay you to be my valet, if you liked, although if you joined the crew you'd have very few costs."

"Cedric, I-"

I cut him off before he could turn me down. "You don't have to decide anything right now, and of course I don't expect you to return my sentiments, but I wanted you to know. I'm happy for us to still be friends, and most likely you'd have to be... all right with seeing me with others as well, because it's complicated, and I can't go into too many details, but."

Oliver stood up, took a breath and swiped his glasses off his face, polishing them briefly on his shirt before putting them back on.

"Cedric, you really are impossible. You've always been impossible, and somehow after your ordeal, you've managed to become even more impossible than before."

I swallowed, then stood up too, as it seemed the thing to do. "I... yes, I know."

Then he placed his hands on my cheeks and kissed me on the lips.

My brain stopped working entirely, and he was pulling away before I realised I had barely kissed him back.

Not willing to let him escape on that note, I grabbed him around the waist and pulled him back in, kissing him properly this time. I poured all the yearning I'd felt over the time we'd known each other into it. When the kiss broke this time, both of us were breathless and Oliver's spectacles had steamed up.

"Oliver, that was wonderful," I said, softly.

"I... I'll have to, I shouldn't have, oh dear," he stammered and then fled the room. I listened as his steps clattered down the stairs and the front door opened and closed.

I took a seat on the bed, rubbed a hand over my warm cheek and exhaled.

"That could have gone a lot worse, I suppose..."

CHAPTER 31

IN WHICH CEDRIC RETURNS TO SEA

I took Father's carriage down to the docks, loaded with my trunk, and a few extra suitcases. Saying farewell to Mother had been hard, but I think hinting that there was a limited amount of trouble I could get into on a ship under the watchful eye of Sir Gabriel convinced her. Then she convinced Father, who was still well charmed by Gabriel following the dinner party. I'd sent word to Oliver at his flat, letting him know the details of the sailing, but I wasn't sure if I expected him to do anything about it, he'd not been in touch since our encounter in my room.

Wanting Oliver to be brave and come down to the ship wouldn't make it happen though.

I had found the house a little stifling, in the few days I'd been home. Although it was grand to see my parents again, I couldn't help but feel the call to do more, the very call that had led to my poor behaviour in the past and the reasons for my being sent away in the first place.

I missed Gabriel and Dante as well. I had become used to sleeping next to Gabriel, and I worried a little about how Dante was feeding...

Well, at least I'd soon be back with them. Using Gabriel's

double identity had worked beautifully, although in the off chance that Oliver *did* show up, it would require another explanation... but I could deal with that once we were clear of Britain.

My stomach was butterflies at the thought of being alone with Gabriel and Dante again.

Especially since my dreams had been getting strange again. Nothing like as bad as the dancing stars, but definitely not... normal. Being around Dante again would soothe my soul.

I'd also felt less and less safe when I was out on the streets of London.

I'd left the house a few times, to pick up some cakes to surprise Mother. To purchase new parchment and canvas, and some good brushes, and to collect the finished clothes from the tailors... and it had quickly been uncomfortable. There were so many people in London. So very many, and I had no idea of guessing if they were part of the Unknowable Way or not. Every time a stranger looked at me a moment too long, I was convinced they were about to try and abduct me.

There was simply no way to know who was who... I'd even left an undershirt on when the tailor had measured me because I didn't want him to see the tattoo.

No, leaving London was safest for me. We may have got away from them in Casablanca, but I hadn't recognised any of the people there from Kingston, so there was no way to know how big the cult was, how many continents it spanned, and how well in touch with each other they were.

My chest had been getting quite tight as I mused on all this, but it eased a little when the docks came into view and my eyes landed on the Devil's Whore.

The carriage driver, who'd been with the family since I was a boy, pulled up and unloaded the trunk.

I signalled to Marco, who was on lookout at the side of the

ship. He smiled and waved back and soon two crew members had come down to carry my trunk aboard.

Gabriel emerged shortly after and I smiled wide, holding myself back from kissing him right there on the shores of the Thames.

"Welcome back, Cedric," Gabriel said. "It's good to see you."

He handed the driver a coin for his trouble, and I took one of my suitcases in hand. I watched as the carriage moved away and there on the other side of the street was Oliver. Unmistakable in a grey traveling coat and spectacles. He held a suitcase not unlike my own, and had his trusty old leather satchel over his shoulder.

My breath caught.

He saw me and his face lit up, and I'm sure mine did too. I wanted to race to him, wrap my arms around him and kiss the breath out of him, but instead I raised a hand in greeting.

"Gabriel, look, it's Oliver, he's coming too!"

Gabriel had been warned this might happen of course, I'd sent several letters to the ship while I was staying up town.

We'd sort out the details once we were all on board and far from London.

I settled for shaking Oliver's hand, although I was aware my mouth was stretched in a wide smile. "Good to see you, Oliver. This is Captain Gabriel Durant. Captain, my old friend Oliver Stanhope."

They shook hands and Oliver smiled politely. "I hope you don't mind my joining the expedition. Cedric made it sound as if there would be room, and that I wouldn't be imposing."

"Of course not," Gabriel said, shooting me a look at the word 'expedition'. I smiled back at him innocently. "Cedric has spoken very highly of you."

Oliver blushed and nodded, and together we went up the gangplank and onto the ship.

Gabriel gave the order to cast off, and soon we left London behind us.

"I'm so glad you decided to come," I said, turning to Oliver.

He gave me a sweet, shy smile and my heart turned over. "I didn't want to miss you, again." He said. "When you disappeared from Kingston, I was beside myself. Word came from town you'd been abducted and I just felt awful, I'd failed you, I'd failed your father, I'd failed..." he trailed off and looked around the deck. "Is there somewhere more private we could be having this conversation by any chance?"

"Of course," I said. I led the way to the captain's cabin, since it was closest to the deck and Marco had left my trunk in there. It was clearly where Gabriel wanted me, which was perfectly to my liking as well.

Oliver looked doubtful. "Isn't this the captain's cabin?"

"Yes," I said. "Please continue."

Oliver looked directly at my trunk and then at me. "You said something about seeing you with others, is this what you meant?"

Oh all right, we're having this conversation immediately. Probably for the best...

"Yes, well, you see, me and the Captain have a sort of arrangement. And Dante, the quartermaster as well. I'm not... I don't want to give them up, but I want you too, I'm sorry, I know that sounds utterly greedy."

Oliver smiled, which was the last expression I expected. He took a seat on the desk chair.

"Cedric, I've ... I used to work for your father, so I squashed down and ignored what I felt for you. I've never felt anything but envy, knowing you were going out and spending time with God knows who. I've seen the lash marks on your back, the bruises on your neck from people's lips. I've wanted to be the one giving you mementoes like that, but I didn't begrudge you getting them."

I sat down on the bed, the wind taken out of me. There was a lot to process in what he'd just said.

"I, oh. All right. That's good?" I ventured. My heart fluttered again, and this time I felt a certain amount of heat in my cock as well. The thought of Oliver, who'd I'd imagined sweet and innocent, recognising what the marks on me were... The thought of him with a leather strap, delivering discipline. I got slightly light-headed.

"I know you well enough to know you'd never be satisfied with just one lover for the rest of your days," Oliver said. "I've made my peace with it. The captain and Dante, well, they're handsome, I see the appeal. Perhaps I'd be willing to join in sometimes, but you'll have to let me take things slowly."

"Slowly, yes of course," I nodded. My mouth was dry now.

"Is there a cabin for me?" he asked hopefully.

"I expect so."

"Right, well, I might go and settle in, but first, Cedric..." Then he pounced on me. There really is no other word for it. One moment he was on the chair, and I was sitting up on the bed, and the next he'd flattened me on the bed and was kissing me with a ferocity I didn't know he had in him. I returned it gladly, because this I knew what to do with. I put my hands on his ass and pulled him closer and he ground down on me, making me moan with need.

This continued for a glorious minute or so and then he sat up, wiped his mouth on his sleeve and got off the bed. "Let's reconvene at a later hour, shall we?"

He readjusted his glasses, wiped his hands off in a businesslike manner and was gone.

What the fuck have I got myself into?

CHAPTER 32

IN WHICH CEDRIC SETTLES INTO LIFE ON
THE DEVIL'S WHORE

*O*nce I'd pulled myself together, as much as I could manage, I went back out on deck and found Dante. He turned and smiled at me.

"Welcome back," he said. Then he slipped his arm around me and we shared a kiss.

"Thank you, it's good to be back." I pressed against his side and just enjoyed the feel of him against me. "I hope you haven't been starving yourself..." I ventured.

"Of course not," he said. "London has a fine vampire community and I ate very well indeed."

For a moment I felt a swell of jealousy, but it ebbed just as quickly as it had swelled. I just needed to hear one thing to feel good again. "But nothing tasted as good as me, did it?"

He laughed, soft and low. "No, Cedric. There's no one like you." He leaned in and kissed the top of my head, which made my heart warm and happy.

I'd said I love you to the both of them, I'd thought, on that night when they'd rescued me. But I'd been almost all the way asleep when it had happened, and I hadn't felt brave enough to say it again since. The stars knew neither of them had said it to me, either.

I almost felt like I could say it then, but the moment passed.

"I think Oliver and I need some alone time tonight," I said.

"Very good. I believe Gabriel is showing him to his cabin at the moment," Dante said. "It's right next to mine, for reference."

"How convenient. I'm looking forward to you all getting to know each other." I went up on my toes and kissed him softly. "I hope it all works out."

"I expect if anyone can make it work, you can."

Gabriel re-emerged then, and I squeezed against Dante and then let go of him to say a proper hello to Gabriel.

We had left London behind by this point, so there was no fear of being seen by curious townsfolk. Not that it necessarily would have stopped me at that point, I was exalting in the freedom of the ship.

Gabriel lifted me in his arms and kissed me soundly. He set me back down before speaking.

"Interesting boy, that Oliver of yours," he said. There was a twinkle in his eye. "He wanted some details of what I had done with you, and when I mentioned the shackles, and that memorable night we spent playing with rope before we landed in London, he became positively animated. I believe in the next few weeks the three, or perhaps four of us will have a very amusing time. If Dante is interested I mean."

My trousers were entirely too tight and I swallowed hard, shifting my legs apart a little so I could give myself a little more space.

"Oh, well, is that so?" I asked. Then I let myself smile with all the joy in my heart. "I can't wait. I think it'll just be me and Oliver tonight though, we have some catching up to do."

"Yes, he was very clear on that point as well." Gabriel ruffled his hand through his hair. "You be good now, puppy."

"I don't know how," I said, and winked at him. "But I do think I ought to rest up before tonight. Wake me for dinner?"

"I'm the captain of this ship," Gabriel said. "I have better things to do than run around after your pert little ass." I pulled back from him, my hand flying to my chest in mock dismay.

"Well, you did *rescue* my pert little ass," I said, giving it a little wiggle as I turned away. "And I expect you to do all sorts of things to it tomorrow, Captain."

I let myself into the captain's cabin, kicked off my boots and collapsed onto the bed, sighing with happiness at the familiar smell.

I was out like a light.

Suddenly I was back on the deck, and the full moon was setting on the horizon, and the stars were above me. Close enough to touch, bright white that almost hurt to look upon.

And behind the stars, something moving, a dark shadow in the velvet blackness.

I tore my eyes from the stars to look around me. Hooded figures ringed me, holding candles in front of them. I couldn't see the details of any of their faces.

There was a noise and it took me a moment to distinguish it from the dull roar of the ocean waves. It was chanting, they were ringed around me and chanting, just as they had in Casablanca.

The skin of my back tautened and stung. It was so sudden and so intense I cried out, and when there was another yanking sensation, I crumpled to my knees. I threw my head back to see the stars, two of them pulling inexorably apart and making way for whatever horror there was behind it.

"No!" I shouted, as loudly as I could. One of the cultists approached me, candle held out to the side. They had something else in their other hand.

"Here, Chosen One, this will ease your pain, take it."

If I'd been awake I never would have taken it, but in the dream it made sense to take it from them. I closed my hand around whatever it was and the tattoo on my back moved, which was the worst sensation of all.

I woke up, panting into the pillow.

The door to the cabin slammed open and Dante came in, his eyes wide. "It happened again, didn't it?"

"Ugh, yes," I said. I rolled over onto my side and looked up at him. "Worse than before. It didn't happen at all like that in London."

"Perhaps they link you to the ship," he said, sitting beside me and stroking my forehead with his cool hand. "It could be they're casting spells that will only work while you're on the Whore."

I pulled a face. "Well, I hate that. This ship is where I want to be, but I don't want any more of those dreams."

"Perhaps we ought to have got you another witch's charm in London," he mused. Then his eyes dropped to my hand, which I had fisted at my side. "What have you got there?"

"What? I don't have..." But he was right, I had something clutched in my hand. With a growing sense of horror, I slowly unfurled my fingers, revealing a strange thing. It was a crude human form carved out of mahogany, with no facial features. But there was something etched into its back. The symbol seemed to have an eye at the centre and weird curling tendrils coming out symmetrically to each side.

"That's... it looks like your tattoo," Dante said, his voice so low I almost couldn't hear it.

To be continued...

If you enjoyed this book, please leave a review on Amazon. Indie authors rely on star ratings and reviews to go up the algorithm and be seen by more readers.

Keep a weather eye on the horizon for Cedric's next story, coming soon!

Sign up for Drake's newsletter for updates on new releases
https://www.subscribepage.com/q4c4n0
Come join Drake's Crew reader's group to meet other fans and get exclusive content – maybe
you'll even get to name – or become! – a character in the next book
https://www.facebook.com/groups/1272511269588779/

Find Drake online:
Twitter: https://twitter.com/DrakeLamarque
Pinterest: https://www.pinterest.nz/drakelamarque/
Newsletter: https://www.subscribepage.com/q4c4n0
BookBub: https://www.bookbub.com/profile/drake-lamarque
Instagram: https://www.instagram.com/drakelamarque/

ACKNOWLEDGMENTS

As always, my beloved by many names, my emo vampire demon darling. Thank you for everything.

To K and L, my beta readers. Your cheerleading and careful corrections are invaluable. I couldn't do this without you.

And to the members of Drake's Crew. Thank you for trying out this new venture into a new part of Gideon's universe, and I hope you love Cedric as much as you loved Gideon. Thanks for all your support!

GENTLEMAN'S BOUNTY

BOOK 2 - VAMPIRE'S INDULGENCE

Buy Now

Unfortunately for Cedric Hale-Harrington, ignoring a curse doesn't make it go away. Especially when it's tattooed on his back.

After a close escape from the cult who want to sacrifice him, Cedric is happily aboard the Devil's Whore, staying close to his lovers, the dashing and dominant Captain Lucifer, the mysterious vampire Dante and his former tutor Oliver.

By rights, it should be a party all night, every night, But his dreams are getting steadily stranger, and he's brought something back from one of them. When bounty hunters start relentlessly pursuing the ship it looks like Cedric can't ignore the claim the cult has on him.

The Cult of the Unknowable Way draws ever closer and they aren't about to let him sail off into the sunset, not when they have a dark and potentially world-ending plan for him.

Vampire's Indulgence is a gay harem MMMM romance, book 2 in a 4 book series. There's a Happy Ever After at the end of the series. This book features sharing, consensual kink and a dash of Lovecraftian horror.

HIS PIRATICAL HAREM

BOOK ONE – CABIN BOY

Buy now

I've never been what I was supposed to be. Wealthy sons of Port Governors aren't supposed to be ejected from the British Navy after less than a year, they're not supposed to like pulp romances or daydream about the handsome heroes of the stories instead of the heroines.

When my Father issued me an order to marry a woman, I knew I had no choice but to make my own way in the world, and I found a berth on the first ship out of Jamaica.

I didn't mean to join a pirate ship, and I certainly didn't intend to find myself the cabin boy to an incredibly charming Pirate Captain. Or that I'd also be attracted to the mysterious First Mate, or that both of them would show me all sorts of unspeakable and salacious pleasures while on board. How can I choose just one of them when I want both?

In addition to confusion on board the ship, there's also enchanting genderfluid merfolk, a cat which seems to understand a lot more than it should, an unseasonable storm and a sea witch with a serious grudge... and with all these complications, I am definitely in over my head.

~

Come and meet the crew:

Gideon: an innocent with a lot of forbidden desires and a lot of love to give

Tate: a huge, muscular ship's captain with a sweet side

Ezra: a dominant and closed off first mate

Ora: a genderqueer, curious and affectionate merman

HIS PIRATICAL HAREM

BOOK TWO – FIRST MATE'S PET

Buy now

Things were looking good, until the ship's cat became a man...

I didn't mean to join a pirate ship, but now that I'm here, well. Life is pretty good. Between the sexy and intimidating Captain Tate, the mysterious First Mate, Ora the merfolk and now Zeb the ship's cat I'm well entertained.

Rumours abound that the Royal Navy are searching for me at my father's order, and between that, an eventful trip to Tortuga (the famed pirate town) and maintaining the relationships with the crew... I've certainly got my work cut out for me.

∾

Meet the crew:

Gideon: a well bred young man who is discovering his forbidden desires aren't necessarily a problem at sea

Tate: the impressive Captain with a sweet side
Ezra: the controlling and alluring First Mate
Ora: a genderqueer, sweet and mystical merman
Zeb: a cat shifter, who's learning about being human

HIS PIRATICAL HAREM

BOOK THREE - MERFOLK'S MATE

Buy now

The British Navy caught up to the Grey Kelpie, and everything I'd built for my life has fallen apart.

Tate and Ezra are headed for the gallows. Ora has disappeared into an unwelcome sea and I have no idea what's become of the ship's cat...

It's up to me to save them, but I'm trapped on the Naval ship, the same as my lovers. If I'm to get us out of here, I'm going to have to use all my wits, and maybe a little magic?

$\sim$

Meet the crew:

Gideon: a well-bred young man discovering a new side of himself

Tate: the sweet Captain with a dark past

Ezra: a dominating First Mate who's slowly finding his soft side

Ora: a mystical merfolk who understands more than the rest

Zeb: an affectionate cat shifter who knows what he wants

~

Content warning: some knife and blood play in one scene

HIS PIRATICAL HAREM

BOOK FOUR - CAPTAIN'S TREASURE

Buy now

I, Gideon Keene, have two big problems.

Two things, well, people, standing between me and my
happiness.

One is a vengeful sea witch called Solomon, who has it in for me
and my beloved Captain Tate.

The other is my father.

One has found us, the other is hounding us. It's time to take the
battle to them, hold my head high and fight first one, then the
other.

But how can a cabin boy, a ship's cat, a member of the merfolk
and two pirates defeat the most powerful sea witch in the
Caribbean? Tate betrayed him, badly, years ago and now his
furious magic has drawn our ship to his blasted islands.

Assuming we survive, then take on the governor of Jamaica, who is determined to see me married to a nice girl and producing heirs?

This is going to take all the courage I have, all the magic I can summon to me, and the wits and understanding of each of my cherished lovers. Not one of us could do it alone, but maybe... just maybe, we can do it together.

ALSO PUBLISHED BY GREY KELPIE STUDIO

RIVAL PRINCES BY JAXON KNIGHT

Buy now

There are three golden rules for new recruits at Fairyland Theme Park:

1. No breaking character, even if you're dying of heat exhaustion
   2. Always give guests the most magical time
   3. No falling in love.

Nate's only been at work one day, and he's already broken all three.

Fast-tracked into a Prince role, Nate's at odds with Dash, the handsome not-so-charming prince who is supposed to be training him. Nate doesn't know how he ended up on Dash's bad side, but the broody prince sure is hot when he gets mad.

Dash has worked long and hard to play Prince Justice at Fairyland. Now, instead of focusing on his own performance, he is forced to train newbie Nate to be the perfect prince. Nate's annoying ease with the guests coupled with his charm and good looks could dethrone Dash from his number one spot ... so why does he secretly want to kiss him?

Fairyland heats up as sparks fly between the two rival princes. Will they get their fairytale romance before they're kicked out of Fairyland for good?

Find out in this standalone MM contemporary romance by Jaxon Knight, set in an amusement park where fairytales can come true.

ALSO PUBLISHED BY GREY KELPIE STUDIO

MISCHIEF AND MAYHEM BY JAXON KNIGHT

Buy now

Mischief

Protecting royalty at Fairyland theme park seemed about as far from Afghanistan as Cody could get. But the hot new rollercoaster brings up some unexpected trouble - and not the kind of trouble he knows how to handle alone.

Mayhem

Dean loves running the Spaceship Mayhem roller coaster - he gets to meet new people every day! When he sees a handsome, troubled security guard repeatedly fail to ride it, he sees an opportunity to help. And maybe they can be more than friends?

Cody reluctantly accepts cute, boy-next-door Dean's help and sparks fly between them, but between mischief, mayhem and miscommunication, can they ever make a relationship work?

Mischief and Mayhem is a slow burn, opposites attract MM sweet romance featuring snark, foolishness, motorbikes, assumptions, the chicken door and a HEA

ALSO PUBLISHED BY GREY KELPIE
STUDIO

RECIPE FOR CHAOS BY JAXON KNIGHT

Buy now

The recipe is simple:
    Charlie cooks an amazing meal
    Charlie impresses heir to the theme park Max Jones
    Charlie gets a promotion and a dash of control over his
kitchen

But the perfect recipe becomes unpalatable with one wrong
ingredient and Max Jones is not behaving how Charlie
expected...

Max is meant to inherit the entire Fairyland theme park but he
just wants to party, have fun and bed as many people as possible.
That is, until he meets Charlie and falls for him so hard he can't
even finish the delicious meal.

Charlie doesn't have time for clubs or helicopter flights over the
city, but Max is accustomed to getting what he wants, and he
wants Charlie.

Featuring one part Billionaire, one part sensible chef, six cups of attraction, a generous dose of snark and a freshly prepared Happy Ever After.

THE GOOD, THE BAD AND THE DAD BY JAXON
KNIGHT

Buy now

Haru is a single dad, a widower, doing his best to balance his career and raising his little girl, Minako. Thankfully Fairyland theme park is a haven for both of them. However, when both a prince and a pirate start courting Haru, his balancing act gets a lot harder...

Cillian plays a pirate at Fairyland theme park and he loves playing the roguish character in and out of work hours. The last thing he wants is to settle down with a guy with a kid, so can't he stop thinking about handsome single dad Haru. And why can't he stop looking at pictures of Prince Magnificence and his stupid symmetrical face? And why does he keep running into both of them?

Grayson feels he's found his home in the role of Prince Magnificence, but he's more likely to run from love than seek it out. Until he meets Haru, that is. Christmas is complicated by Grayson's role being featured in a special Christmas celebration. Not only that, but his feelings for Haru, and his possible rival

Cillian keep on growing. Maybe it's time to stop hiding who he really is?

The Good, the Bad and the Dad is a sweet MMM romance featuring a single father, a rogue and a trans prince with a heart of gold. No cheating, just the tentative first steps into polyamory.

Printed in Great Britain
by Amazon

55602595R00121